KIMBERLY VAN METER

Cold Case Reunion

ROMANTIC
SUSPENSE

Recycling programs
for this product may
not exist in your area.

ISBN-13: 978-0-373-27739-1

COLD CASE REUNION

Books by Kimberly Van Meter

KIMBERLY VAN METER

wrote her first book at sixteen and finally achieved publication in December 2006. She writes for Harlequin Superromance and Harlequin Romantic Suspense. She and her husband of seventeen years have three children, three cats and always a houseful of friends, family and fun.

A warrior isn't always the one charging into the fight. Sometimes he's the quiet one dispensing wisdom; watching and listening for the right moment to make a difference. This is to my grandfather, Orval Rhoan, a man who throughout my life has always been the quiet, steady source of wisdom, laughter, and really corny jokes that always made me laugh.

Chapter 1

Angelo Tucker remembered stories told at his grandfather's knee of how their tribe used to walk on their hands and fished the mighty Hoh River with their feet until Creator came along to show them a better way.

He and his younger brother Waylon used to laugh out loud at the idea of catching smelt with their toes.

"Why didn't they just walk on their own, Papa?" Waylon asked, his dark eyes gleaming with mirth. They'd loved Papa's stories of the beginnings even if the tales had seemed completely outrageous.

"We were not so wise," Grandfather had answered, smoothing the wild jet-black hair on Waylon's head. "All the blood rushing to our heads clouded our reason. Creator taught us a better way and we were thankful. Aren't you thankful you don't have to fish with your feet?" he asked, his worn face crinkling in a warm, teasing smile.

"Very much, Papa," Waylon had answered fervently. "I don't want to fish with my toes."

"It's just a story, Waylon," Angelo had scoffed at his younger brother's gullibility, earning a subtle frown from Papa. "Creator isn't real and no one would really walk on their hands all their life. It's not possible anyway."

"It is so true." Waylon had pushed Angelo, a fierce scowl on his young face. He turned to Papa for reinforcement, although there was a hint of a question in his expression, for Angelo was his big brother and his idol. "Right, Papa? Tell Angelo he's wrong."

Papa, the hereditary tribal chief, took a long moment to answer. Angelo had shifted under Papa's deep, assessing stare; it felt as if it had zeroed in on his very soul, and then Papa had said, "White Arrow...you have much to learn about your people. Your eyes are closed, but when the time is right, they will open. In the meantime, do not mock your brother for what you refuse to see."

"Yeah," Waylon echoed, the laughter returning to his voice as he tackled Angelo, taking both to the worn carpet of their grandfather's living room.

The memory of that day crashed through Angelo's mind now with all the violence of a head-on collision, and the unexpected pain brought him back to the present more quickly than the sound of his partner's voice. She repeated the facts as they knew them as they drove to the local facility where the body was being held. He'd known returning to the reservation wasn't going to be a picnic but he hadn't been prepared for the mental assault he'd undergone the moment he stepped foot on native soil.

When his partner, Grace Kelly, a woman who was

nothing like her famous namesake in appearance or disposition, noted his attention had wandered, she lowered the case file to her lap to stare him down. "Please let me know if I'm interrupting your quiet time."

"Settle down, Kelly," he retorted irritably as the urgent care facility came into view. He was dealing with more than the case but he wasn't in the mood to share. "I was listening."

"Yeah, I could tell," Grace said dryly, returning to the case file with a sigh. "The body was bagged at the scene by the locals. We can only hope everything was done right. I would've been more comfortable if our forensics team had collected the evidence. Agent Byron Hicks went missing about a week ago, according to his wife. The body was identified by a fingerprint match." She scanned the page, adding, "Says here Hicks was found by a man named Sam Fisher on the bank of the Hoh River with a single bullet wound to the back of the head." She pursed her lips and shook her head at the mystery. "Helluva way to end a vacation. Wife said he came up here to do some salmon-fishing. Looks like he caught more than he planned."

Angelo refrained from comment as his grip tightened on the steering wheel, but his mind kept detouring in spite of his best efforts. There was a reason he had never returned, not for visits, not for anything. The weight of his ancestors' judgment seemed to press on him though he told himself repeatedly he'd done nothing wrong in leaving. Not everyone's path started and ended at the reservation. At least that's what he'd tried to tell his grandfather. He bit back a sigh and ignored the stab of guilt that always followed when he allowed his thoughts to wander too closely to his memories of living here.

The urgent care facility, with its bare, utilitarian construction, was as ugly as it ever had been because there had never been enough money for cosmetic improvements. Not having enough money…a common thread that wove its way through the reservation. If he'd stayed it would've been his responsibility to look after the tribe, to sit in on the pointless tribal meetings with the government, fighting and scrabbling for the scraps from the white man's table. His tribe had not followed the casino route as had so many of their tribal brothers and therefore, money was always scarce.

As they exited the car he wondered who had taken over the administration position after Hector had died. The fact that he was clueless about who was in charge illuminated just how removed he was from the place. And yet, everything looked the same, locked in time.

Grace swiped at her nose. The moist, chilly air common to the Pacific Northwest at nearly all times of the year made her shiver in her trench coat. "You grew up here?" When Angelo nodded, she offered a grim analysis. "It's cold, wet and creepy. It must've been a friggin' fairy tale calling this patch of dirt home."

"It had its moments," he said, his sharp gaze taking in everything at once. The last time he'd walked through these doors he'd been summoned to identify his baby brother's body. Waylon had been sixteen when someone had shot him in the back, but the fall into the river was what had killed him. The official cause of death was drowning. Like Hicks, Waylon's body had been hauled from the Hoh. The murder had never been solved. Waylon's death had crippled their grandfather mentally. A year later, Papa had walked into the forest and tumbled down a ravine, breaking his neck. And just like that, Angelo's last remaining family member was gone, leaving him completely alone. An uncomfortable tremble shook his frame and he was glad for the bulk of his trench coat for cover. After that day he'd sworn he'd never walk through these doors again. And until this moment, he'd kept that vow.

"Is it weird to be back?" Grace asked, breaking the silence as they walked through the back door of the urgent care, their shoes scraping against the aged and faded tiles.

"A little," he lied, his gaze taking in the surroundings with one sweep. Only a few lights lit the darkened facility, but as the hairs rose on his neck and goose pimples erupted, his stare locked on a woman who emerged from a side office, her dark hair pulled into a short serviceable ponytail that twitched with the brisk clip of her stride.

His gaze feasted even as he took a mental step away. If the memory of his brother's murder made the visit home unpalatable, running into Mya Jonson only made it worse.

Heaven help him, but time hadn't been unkind. If anything, maturity had molded what had been considered a pretty face into one that now stopped traffic. Her dark eyes burned, saying all the things those tightly compressed, gorgeous lips wouldn't. A wave of anger and hostility from her hit him, leaving little to guesswork as to how she felt about seeing him again. He wouldn't say he'd spent the last fifteen years pining for his lost love, but he couldn't rightly say he'd forgotten her, either. Seeing Mya again only served to freshen what he'd hoped had gone stale inside his heart. Still, they both had jobs to do and he wouldn't allow the past to get in the way; he hoped she felt the same. There was only one way to see how this reunion would play out.

"Hello, Mya," he said, inclining his head in a stiff greeting.

"Angelo," she acknowledged, equally stiff.

"Gotta love these hometown reunions," Grace muttered beneath her breath before extending her hand to Mya. "Special Agent Grace Kelly, FBI," she said in introduction.

Mya's gaze moved to Grace as if only too happy to look away from Angelo and visibly thawed as she accepted the gesture. "Mya Jonson, I'm the resident doctor here at Healthy Living. Unfortunately, our regular coroner is on a much-needed vacation so you'll have to bring in your own team for an autopsy."

Angelo processed the info silently. A doctor... She'd always been whip-smart. A surge of pride that he had no business feeling filled his chest. He'd known she had what it took to make something of herself. The fact that she'd left the reservation, attained an education and then returned even though she could've made a higher wage elsewhere spoke volumes as to where her heart remained: with the tribe.

Well, seems that much hadn't changed about her.

"We already have a team assembling. We just need somewhere to hold the body for the time being to preserve any trace evidence that may have been left behind," Angelo said, noting the subtle differences in the woman he'd once loved but had walked away from so many years ago.

"Of course," Mya said, gesturing down the hall. "Follow me."

"You cut your hair," he murmured, almost to himself, catching a quick, narrowed stare from Grace that caused him to flush.

Mya didn't even give him a cursory glance as she

answered, moving briskly down the hall to their destination. "I've done many things in the last fifteen years."

The vague answer did little to soften her meaning. His comment had been too personal and he knew it. He shouldn't have mentioned it, but it'd just popped out of his mouth before he realized what a mistake it would be. Her reaction told him there would be no polite conversation between them. He ought to be grateful. He found polite conversation trite and useless. But Mya's hair... he had distinct memories of those silken black strands sliding through his fingers, and now, judging by the abbreviated ponytail, it looked as if it'd been chopped to her shoulders...he found himself lamenting the loss.

Mya stepped aside and gestured at an open door. "Here is the morgue. It's not large but it has a cold-storage locker that should meet your needs. Do you know when your pathologist is set to arrive?"

"Not until the morning," Grace answered. "We'll hole up here for the night if that's all right with you. Any hotels you could recommend?"

"We don't have hotels for outsiders," she said, sliding her gaze to Angelo. "Perhaps the next town over has some vacancies."

Grace stared quizzically at Mya, not quite sure what to make of her answer. Angelo smirked at Mya, minutely shaking his head. This was the reason the rez was dying on the vine. Damn tribe was always cutting off its nose to spite its face. Mya's attitude was an apt reminder of why he was thankful every day that he'd chosen to leave. "Don't worry, my family's got a place here. We can stay there. It's not the Hilton but it has running water and a roof," he told Grace, ignoring Mya's thinned lips and the flash in her dark eyes.

"Are you sure you wouldn't feel more at home in a hotel?" she asked.

"Oh, I'd likely feel right at home in a hotel, but we'll stay here," he said easily. He didn't relish the idea of going home after all this time, but Mya was right, there were no vacancies for outsiders and, to date, that included him. But it made more sense to stay here because this was where the investigation would be focused, and since he didn't imagine he'd enjoy sleeping in the Range Rover, he was willing to go home for the time being. Besides, it was temporary and he could handle temporary.

"I suppose that's your right," she said coolly.

"Yes, it is." Why was he baiting her? He didn't know. He shifted and caught Grace's pointed gaze, and he knew he better cut it out if he wanted to keep his past with Mya private. Grace was a bulldog when it came to sniffing out details other people wanted to remain hidden. And he wasn't fool enough to believe she'd blunt those skills just because he was the one in her line of sight.

"While you two play catch-up I'm going to take a look at the body." Grace shot him a dark look that promised plenty of questions later and then disappeared out the door.

Uncomfortable silence stretched between them and Angelo wished he'd taken the initiative to get out of there sooner. Mya lifted her chin and broke the silence first. "I want to say this and get it out into the open. You mean nothing to me, Angelo. Don't ask me personal questions, like about my hair or who I'm dating. I will work with you in a professional capacity, but anything other than that is out of the question. I'm over you."

"After fifteen years I'd hope so," he murmured, but her words stung.

She ignored his jab and continued, her voice low but strong. "I'm telling you this because I feel obligated to warn you. There are others here who won't be so accommodating."

"If anyone refuses to cooperate I'll have them arrested for obstruction," he said, his jaw tensing.

"You'll do what you feel is necessary, what is best for you," she countered evenly. Unspoken was her belief that Angelo *always* did what was best for him. He bit back swear words, hating how ten minutes spent with Mya could heap a ten-pound weight of guilt on his shoulders. The fact that he had nothing to feel guilty for sharpened his voice.

"Yes, I will. I'm here to investigate the murder of a fellow agent. I don't care what anyone thinks of me, including you. Thanks for the heads-up, but I don't need it. People will cooperate or they'll go to jail. Simple as that."

Her smile called him a fool. "All right then. The clinic opens at 8:00 a.m. and I have a full case load. Iris will see to your needs, should you have any."

"Iris Beaudoin?" he asked.

"Yes."

He filed that away. Iris had never been able to govern her mouth and pretty much said whatever popped into her head. He resisted the urge to pinch the bridge of his nose as a headache pulsed to life behind his eyes. Just the thought of having Iris as his go-between caused pain to erupt. He had to ask, "Is Iris the same as I remember her?"

At that Mya's smile widened but her eyes were deadly cold. "Yes. Worse perhaps."

Great.

"Body is secure," Grace called out, and the sound of a closing door followed.

Mya didn't wait for his say-so and started shutting the clinic again, double-checking the locks and doors before heading down the hallway to the exit.

He followed, barely clearing the door before she closed and locked it. She was nearly to her car, no good-byes, no backward glance, when he called out to her.

"It doesn't have to be this way," he said, spreading his hands in a gesture of peace.

She paused, her silhouette outlined against the milky light of the one parking-lot lamp. She cut a striking figure in the brisk spring night, her breath curling before her. "It is what it is and we should leave it that way," she answered and then climbed into her car before he could offer a rebuttal.

He watched as she drove away, and even though Grace was waiting for him in the Rover, he stared after her disappearing taillights, wishing for the briefest of moments for a glimpse into the private theater of Mya Jonson's thoughts. He wondered what he'd see.

His instincts told him that he wouldn't like it.

Mya had always been a terrible liar. Her feelings reflected quite clearly in her strong gaze and, assuming that aspect of her hadn't changed, there was no mistaking how she felt about him.

And it wasn't nice.

Chapter 2

By the time Mya made it home, her nerves were a mess. Her plans for a bath had been completely trashed. There was no way she could soak in a tub with her thoughts in such a turbulent, chaotic tangle. Instead, she stripped bare and grabbed her yoga mat, flipping it out on the floor beside the large living-room window, under the full bath of the moon.

But before she could start, her cell phone rang; it was her best friend and lead nurse, Iris. Mya considered letting it go to voice mail, but she knew Iris would only keep calling, so she answered.

"So?"

"So what?" Mya asked.

"Don't be coy. How was your meeting with Angelo?"

"How'd you know— Oh forget it. I swear you have a network to rival the CIA." If Iris knew, for certain Mya's older brother, Sundance, knew as well, since he and Iris were a couple. She was surprised Sundance hadn't driven down to the clinic to welcome Angelo home with a five-knuckle sandwich. "You missed your calling, you know. You should've been a nosy reporter for all the gossip you traffic in."

"Yeah, yeah, get to the good stuff," Iris said impatiently. "Did you let loose and tell him what a jerk he is?"

"Of course not," Mya answered, though she wished she could've. "We were both acting in a professional capacity. I couldn't very well turn into a teenager and start yelling at him for breaking my heart so many years ago."

"Why not?" Iris grumbled. "Hey, did you at least tell him that no one has forgotten?"

"Yes. I also told him that you were going to be his liaison at the hospital should he need anything."

"Fabulous," Iris said, with too much delight. "Can I tell him off for you?"

"No. You'll be the professional I know you are and treat him with courtesy."

"Mya, I love you dearly, but you suck the fun out of everything sometimes," Iris groused but didn't continue to press her agenda. Instead she switched gears, and Mya almost wished she'd stayed on the Angelo-is-scum track. "So, does he look the same?"

"Mostly," Mya admitted grudgingly. "Older, more mature."

"Not fat? How about bald?"

"No and no. Fit as ever with a full head of hair." Those native cheekbones combined with maturity cut a sharp facial plane that was both striking and intimidating. She imagined he used that to his advantage when dealing with criminals. Angelo's nearly black irises gave him an intensity that had never failed to send dark thrills chasing down her nerve endings. It had been almost feral, the way he'd looked at her at times. Was it any wonder she'd found it difficult to find anyone to fill his shoes? She swallowed and realized her breath had become shallow as memories of his touch escaped her control. "He looks the same, only older," she said quickly, hoping Iris didn't notice the catch in her voice, and if she did, would simply chalk it up to fatigue.

"That's too bad," Iris said. "It might be easier to stay away from him if he were bald, fat and missing a few teeth."

Mya chuckled at the image, though it was hard to imagine Angelo letting himself go to hell. He was too focused, too determined to be in control to let something as personal as his physical appearance go downhill. "That's hardly necessary. I won't have any trouble keeping my distance. I have plenty to keep myself occupied with my regular schedule, much less this new complication of a dead agent and an old boyfriend to deal with."

"Wow. Angelo has been downgraded from former fiancé to old boyfriend. Nice touch," Iris said approvingly, but then her tone sobered as she said, "Listen, you can tell everyone else whatever you want, but I remember what you were like when he left. He was more than a boyfriend and he broke your heart."

Iris had a point. Angelo Tucker had shattered her heart into a million pieces, but what did it matter now? The past was dead. Just like their baby. She flinched at the spasm that never failed to hit her whenever she thought of the miscarriage that took the life from her womb, and she rubbed at the sting in her eyes, which she blamed on exhaustion. "Iris, I'm beat. I was about to go to bed if you don't mind," she said, faking a yawn. She was too keyed up to actually sleep, but neither did she want to field further questions from Iris. "I'll see you first thing tomorrow morning."

"But—"

"Good night, Iris." Mya smiled as she heard Iris sputtering even as she clicked off. She loved Iris, but sometimes she was as bull-headed as Sundance, and it would take more energy than she wanted to expend to deal with her at the moment. Besides, she had more pressing issues at hand.

She needed to settle her thoughts and quiet her mind if she was going to get through this time with Angelo on the reservation. She said a quiet prayer to Great Spirit for clarity and then focused on her yoga poses to achieve some type of serenity. She often caught a little flack from Iris for her penchant to do yoga in the nude, but she found clothes binding when she performed her poses. It was mentally freeing to stand under the moonlight naked, bending and stretching her body as her mind emptied of everything but her muscles and her breathing.

Angelo... His name floated through her thoughts unwelcome. Intruding on her attempts at calm, at peace. She tried harder. He looked good. Perhaps rougher around the edges from whatever life experiences he'd collected, but good nonetheless. He probably had women falling over him with those exotic facial features. He'd kept in shape, from what she could tell. There didn't seem to be anything soft about him, not around the middle or his jawline. She exhaled slowly, eyes closed, forcing Angelo from her mind.

Except, he remained. She folded on her mat and

gazed up at the moon, wishing for more strength than she had at the moment.

She'd thought of this moment many times since he'd left the reservation, wondered how she'd handle the pressure and the pain, but nothing compared to the real deal. He still had the power to make her heart stutter. When she could stomach it, she'd imagined—briefly— how their lives might've been different if he'd stayed.

Her hands strayed to her smooth, flat belly. No life there any longer. But once…fifteen years ago, a tiny person had begun to grow. She and Angelo had created a miracle.

And Angelo had never even known she was pregnant.

She sighed and climbed to her feet, annoyed at herself for allowing her thoughts to go down that road. Miscarriages happened all the time. As a doctor she saw them frequently, particularly with the mothers who received little to no prenatal care. She hadn't expected it to happen to her.

But she'd been young and hardly ready to be a mother so she tried to remember that Great Spirit always had her best interests at heart even if it had hurt like hell when it'd happened.

She padded to the bathroom, comfortable in her nakedness in her own home. She owned acres of land so peeping neighbors weren't an issue. She even had a slate-tiled outdoor shower for the summer nights when she used her sweat lodge.

Peace would not find her tonight so she gave up trying. Her mind fought with memories, pain, loneliness and anger.

She wished Porter was here; he'd at least distract her. Good, solid, dependable Porter with his unassuming manner and quiet strength. She considered calling him to invite him over for the evening, but, as her hand curled around her cell phone, she reconsidered. Porter would want to talk about the fact that Angelo was here. He, of all people, would have the most to lose. But she didn't want to talk to anyone about Angelo, least of all Porter.

Mya made a sound of disgust at herself and headed for the shower. She was being ridiculous…and shameful.

Angelo turned his back on everything he ever held dear with little regard as to how his actions would affect those around him.

She'd meant what she'd said. She was over him. It didn't matter if he was back. Her heart had closed to him the day he'd abandoned them all.

And yet…

His hand remained clutched around her heart as if in a stranglehold and there was little she seemed able to do about it—even after fifteen years.

Chapter 3

Angelo jiggled the key in the rusted lock, wiggling it to move the antique tumblers, and when it finally unlocked, the door opened with a shriek from hinges that hadn't seen much action in years.

"You really know how to treat a girl, Tucker," Grace remarked wryly, taking in the run-down and forgotten air of the small two-bedroom shack he'd called home his entire life. "This is some dump you've got. It's no wonder you don't come home often."

He shut the door and flipped the lights, bathing the small living room—if you could call it that—with dim, flickering light as he did a quick check of the premises. He didn't figure anyone would make themselves at home in his grandfather's old place, but he'd been gone a long time and he wasn't about to wake up with an unexpected visitor traipsing through his bedroom. Grace rubbed her arms in response to the chill in the house and he went to the closet and found some blankets. He tossed them her way. "I doubt there's any wood for the fireplace. We'll just have to tough it out for tonight," he said by way of apology. She was right—it wasn't the Hilton—but it was dry and it was their only option for the night unless they wanted to take the chance and drive into Forks in the hopes that they might find a vacancy.

Grace caught the blankets and wasted little time shaking them out for any bugs that might be taking up residence in the folds. Case in point, something dark and insect-like tumbled to the worn hardwood-plank floor and she promptly squashed it beneath her booted heel. At least she wasn't squeamish. Nice to see that army infantry training in her background hadn't gone to waste. "So tell me, what's the story with you and the hot doctor chick?" she said, making quick work of creating a cozy bedroll on the old sofa. "I could sense the history between you two even before things got tense."

Angelo thought of the last time he'd seen Mya. Tears had tracked down her cheeks, open anguish reflecting in her stare, yet she'd refused to consider his offer to move with him. And then, knowing her mind was made up, he'd left her behind. His mouth tensed, even though that day had passed into memory so long ago. He'd never understood Mya's stubborn, ingrained loyalty to the tribe, just as she'd never understood his need for independence. He'd walked and she'd stayed…but her presence in his mind and heart haunted him.

"Nothing?" Grace pressed, shucking her boots and lining them up perfectly at the foot of the couch and within easy grabbing distance should the need arise. "I get it. It's private. My guess is that you were an item and things ended badly. When that happens you've got no closure, makes it hard to move on."

Grace's blithe assessment hit too close to home. "I've moved on just fine," he lied coolly. "My advice? Give up the amateur psych evals and just get to sleep. We're out of here at 0700."

She chuckled in spite of his curt reply and climbed into the bedroll, seemingly mindless of the less-than-desirable conditions. She rested her head on her hand as she settled on her side. "You know, for what it's worth, I think she's got closure issues, too. She looked like she didn't know whether she wanted to hit you or kiss you. Or maybe both. I don't know, maybe that was your thing together."

"She hates me," he answered, surprising himself with the flat statement. "The last thing on her mind is kissing me."

"Yeah, maybe you're right. She did seem pretty pissed at you. Is this going to be a problem for the investigation?" she asked, suddenly troubled.

"No." Angelo didn't let anything cloud his judgment. He wasn't about to start now. And he was finished with the conversation. "Oh seven hundred, Kelly, or your ass is walking," he said, then disappeared into the bedroom that had been his grandfather's when he and Waylon were kids.

Safely behind the door, he closed his eyes and inhaled to loosen the tightness squeezing his chest. Perhaps he should've driven into Forks. Just being here had awakened something raw and vulnerable.

The old shack groaned with the wind gusting from the Hoh River and he thought of how Waylon had been scared of the sounds outside when he'd been a little kid until Papa had told him the rustling of the wind was simply *T'ist'ilal,* or Thunderbird, beating his mighty wings. The Thunderbird was the sacred mythic bird that was large enough to carry a whale in its claws.

Waylon, his grandfather, Mya...this place was a minefield of misery.

Even with his eyes closed he found no relief. The Mya in his memory gazed at him with open reproach and sadness; the smooth timbre of Papa's voice echoed in his ear; Waylon's fierce spirit lingered in every dark corner, waiting for him to solve his murder, though, to date, he had not.

His eyes snapped open on a soft groan.

Good God. He never should've returned to this place.

The sure knowledge that Mya felt the same gave him no comfort. Instead, it hurt like hell.

More than he would've imagined after all this time.

He climbed, fully clothed, onto the bed and drew the blanket over him. He knew sleep would be elusive but when it finally found him, his dreams were filled with memories he'd rather forget.

Mya arrived at the clinic, a steaming cup of coffee warming her hand, earlier than the staff so she could open the facility for the FBI team arriving at seven-thirty. She wasn't surprised to see Angelo and his partner waiting at the back entrance. She offered a brief smile to his partner but couldn't find the same courtesy for Angelo. Perhaps if she hadn't slept so fitfully, she might've been more charitable, but the grit burning in her eyes prevented much more civility when it came to Angelo.

"When is your pathologist arriving?" she asked, leading the two to the chilly morgue where the dead agent was being held.

"Eight o'clock," Angelo answered in the same clipped tone. She refrained from glancing at him to surmise if dark circles ringed his eyes as surely as they did her own. "We'll do our best to keep our team out from under your feet."

"Yes. Please see that you do. I have a full day on the calendar and I don't need anything or anyone making it any longer than necessary." She hesitated as a thought came to her. She considered shelving the question but decided against it when she weighed the importance against her personal feelings. "Whom will you be needing to question on the reservation?" she asked, point-blank.

"Sam Fisher, for starters. He found the body," Angelo answered, earning a speculative look from his partner. Perhaps Angelo wasn't supposed to share such details? Mya couldn't be sure, but what she did know was that likely no one on the reservation would take kindly to questioning from Angelo Tucker, nor to his presence. "How long do you think you'll be in town?"

"As long as it takes," he said, though he added, "I hope not long."

She inclined her head and agreed with a murmured, "Yes, let's hope," and continued walking.

Mya felt his stare at her back, but she maintained her stride and pushed open the morgue doors. "I will leave you to your business," she said. "Should you need anything, find Iris. She'll do what she can to assist you."

"Why do I find that hard to believe?" Angelo retorted. She turned and offered him a crisp smile.

"The sooner you solve your case, the sooner you're gone. That's something we all can support. Even Iris."

And then, hiding her trembling hands in the pockets of her white lab coat, she left them behind.

Chapter 4

Barnabus Lipton, aka Dr. Barney, arrived at the clinic, coughing up a lung and holding a hanky to his nose. His disposition, hardly what anyone would call friendly and engaging on his best day, was downright unpleasant as he scowled his way, grumbling under his breath, into the morgue.

"Damn mold spores from all this damp, soggy air... Dragging me all the way here when I hate the coast... Where's this damn body?" he finally barked to Angelo, who gestured to the slab where it lay covered with a white drape. Barney sneezed into his hanky as he walked to the gurney, jerking gloves and facial protection on as he went, and pulled the covering away. Angelo averted his eyes, not particularly squeamish, but in deference to his fellow agent. Dead or not, it didn't sit well with him to stare at the man naked.

"You got everything you need?" he asked Barney,

to which the man grunted an affirmative. "I'll be back in about an hour. Is that enough time to finish your examination?" He received a sneeze in response. "I'll take that as a yes." He jerked his head at Grace. "Let's go. Time to start asking questions."

"Who first?" Grace asked once they'd cleared the morgue. She checked her notes. "Sam Fisher?"

"Yes. He lives on the Hoh River. He used to make his living catching salmon but that was years ago. Not sure he still does, but at least we know where to find him."

However, as they exited the building out the back door, they came face-to-face with someone Angelo wanted to see even less than Mya—her older brother, Sundance Jonson, who, judging by the uniform, was now the tribal police. Fabulous, the man hated him and he carried a gun.

"I wish I'd known they were going to call you. I'd have saved the Bureau the gas money and told them not to bother." Sundance stood beside his Durango, as if knowing Angelo would be coming out that way, his face hard and unforgiving. Angelo swallowed a private sigh of annoyance. Was this a preview of what his time was going to be like here on the rez?

"Sundance," Angelo said, giving the man the barest nod, which wasn't returned. Forget this. They weren't in high school anymore and Angelo wasn't about to play a bunch of stupid posturing games. He started to walk past, but Sundance grabbed his arm, stopping him.

"Get your hand off me," Angelo warned, his voice bordering on a growl. Grace stiffened, her hand snaking to rest lightly on her gun. He put Grace at ease with a glance.

"Or what?" Sundance said, not impressed or swayed.

"Or I'll arrest you for you assaulting a federal agent," Angelo answered coolly. Sundance smirked and dropped his grip, disgust written on every plane of the man's face. "Got something to say to me?" Angelo asked. Oh, yes, the man had plenty to say and Angelo could tell none of it would be nice. He waited, not backing down an inch from that hard stare.

"Stay away from Mya," Sundance said.

So much for keeping the questions to a minimum. There'd be no way in hell Grace would stop digging now. "Cool off, Sundance. I'm not here for anything other than the case."

"So, am I to believe it was just plain bad luck that put you on this case?" Sundance asked, a subtle sneer to his tone.

"Yeah, something like that, but I'd say the bad luck was all mine. Don't you think if I'd wanted to return I would've by now?"

Sundance shrugged. "I wouldn't presume to understand anything you do."

"Fine. Then take it from me, it wasn't my choice to return. Are we through with the pleasantries?"

The weight of Sundance's scrutiny bounced off Angelo's shoulders. He'd long ago stopped caring what anyone from the reservation thought of him, and that included Mya's brother. Sundance evaluated Angelo's statement, and when he decided he believed him, some of the tension loosened from his taut jaw. "You on your way to talk to Sam?"

"Yeah."

"I'll follow you."

"That's not necessary," Angelo said, but Sundance wasn't backing down. He'd already climbed into his

Durango, his mind set. Angelo swore under his breath and stalked to his own vehicle, Grace on his heels.

"Is there anyone on this miserable, wet piece of mud who likes you?" she asked when they'd climbed into the car. He refrained from answering. "That's what I thought. What the hell happened here? I've always believed that old adage, 'still waters run deep,' but I never imagined that you might be the adage personified. You've got some major backstory, my friend, and I can't wait to hear about it."

"There's no backstory worth listening to," he told her, quietly stewing. He and Sundance had never been close but the man seemed to be taking Angelo's return a bit more seriously than the situation warranted. Sundance had practically raised Mya when their alcoholic parents had bit the big one in a car accident, so Angelo had been facing down Sundance when it came to Mya since they were teens. He'd never imagined Sundance would still be this pissed off after fifteen years. Couldn't anyone just let things lie?

"I disagree. I can't wait to see who we run into next who likely wants to put your head on a pitchfork, or whatever it is you Indians do to your enemies."

"I wouldn't know," he muttered. "I never paid much attention to cultural-history lessons."

That'd been Waylon's forte.

Sam Fisher was easy to find, but on a reservation a square mile long, most people were.

"I just found him. I didn't touch nothing and I called right away," Sam said, biting the corner of his lip as if he were afraid the big, bad government was going to string him up for finding a dead agent on his property.

The river churned, swollen with spring runoff, the

heavy current crashing into submerged rocks to erupt in violent spray. Nothing that went into that water was coming out alive, that was for sure. If the body hadn't gotten caught on submerged tree branches, likely Byron Hicks would've washed out to sea.

Angelo roused himself to assure Sam he'd made the right decision. "Everything's going to be all right, Sam. Just tell me what you know. Start from the beginning."

Sam visibly settled, but Angelo could tell he was still shook up over the whole thing. "Nothing much to tell, I just come out here to do some fishing and there he was. At first I thought he'd fallen in somewhere upstream and just floated down here and maybe he was still alive, but when I got closer, he wasn't the right color. He was all blue and pasty and I knew I was looking at a dead man. I called Sundance—he's the law around here since Daniel retired—and I guess they called you when they found out he was an agent." He twisted his fishing cap in his hand, peering up at Angelo to switch subjects. "So, does Mya know you're in town? She's a doctor, you know. Over at the clinic. She's real good, too. Fixed me up when I got a lure stuck in my eyelid. Could've lost my eye," Sam added, arching his brow for emphasis.

"Sorry, Sam. Not here for a reunion."

Sam spared him a speculative look, then shrugged. "Not sayin' nothing, just that she's done good for herself. We're all real proud of her."

Angelo resisted taking the bait. Yes, the entire tribe was proud of Mya and ashamed of him. He got that message loud and clear, always had. But he wasn't about to let Sam's statement get under his skin. Not with Grace standing there soaking up every detail like a mop. Through the years, he'd been careful to keep his private life his own, yet within twenty-four hours of being on the reservation all his dirty laundry was spilling out for everyone to sort through and sniff. "Anything else, Sam?" he asked, adding quickly, "about the case," when the older man looked ready to launch into something unrelated.

"No. That's pretty much it." Sam lifted his shoulders. "Not much I can say. I found him dead and don't know how he got that way. Do you need anything else from me?"

"No. Thanks for your help," Angelo said, noting the subtle shake of Sam's head as he walked away, mumbling something under his breath that Angelo was certain he didn't want to hear. Angelo returned to Grace. He was here to do a job, not play catch-up. Aside from the knowledge that Byron hadn't been on duty when he'd died, there was little else he could find that would provide clues as to what had happened. He'd have to wait until forensics took a look at the trace evidence.

"What the hell was Hicks doing here in the first place?" Grace asked, clear distaste in her expression. The place had a melancholy charm, but only to those who didn't mind being wet most of the time. Having grown up in the dry heat of Arizona, Grace wasn't one of them. She shivered in her coat. "It's not what I'd call a destination spot for vacationing. God, is it always this...dreary?"

"It has good fishing," Angelo said, his gaze drawn to the river once more. Waylon had drowned in this river. Papa used to tell them the Hoh gave them life but it would take it too if they weren't careful. Respect was the key to surviving. What a load of crap. Waylon had respected tradition and he'd still died choking on river water.

"There's lots of places to fish aside from this tiny

reservation," Grace said, her mind focused on the case where his should've been but wasn't. "There had to be something else that drew him here. We ought to ask around."

"Doubtful anyone even gave him the time of day. Whatever he was doing, he was doing on his own."

"So I take it the tribe's not big on tourists?" Angelo's answering smirk caused her to chuckle. "Now I know where you get that sparkling personality of yours."

At that Angelo allowed a small smile. Grace was right, though. While the fishing was decent here, outsiders weren't welcomed with open arms and there were plenty of fishing holes elsewhere with more accommodating neighbors.

"What do we know about Hicks?" he asked, returning to the case.

"Decent agent, nothing on his record that stands out, good or bad. He did his job, kept his head down and clocked out at the end of the day. His wife said he left to go salmon-fishing and never came back. Then your buddy Sam found him dead, washed up on the bank."

"He's not my buddy," Angelo clarified, irked that just because he was from the area, Grace—and everyone else in his department—assumed he was tight with the locals. If they knew the whole truth of it, they'd realize Angelo was the last person the tribe would open up to. Grace was getting the idea, seeing how the reception had been so far, but the cold shoulder was hardly likely to warm up.

In the eyes of the tribe, Angelo was a traitor.

Chapter 5

Mya finished her shift at the clinic and was at her locker changing to go home when Iris, her big, black wolf-hybrid, Saaski, on her heels, found her. Iris never went anywhere without the dog, including work, much to Mya's consternation, but, seeing as Saaski had saved Iris's life when a serial rapist had tried to kill her, Mya turned a blind eye to the dog as long as he didn't bother the patients. "What a day, right?" Iris said, opening her own locker to grab her purse and keys. She reached in her purse to find a treat for Saaski who was waiting patiently for his venison jerky. "I'm still trying to wrap my brain around everything that's happened."

"Yeah, the caseload was pretty heavy. I thought for sure—"

"I'm not talking about the clinic," Iris cut in, annoyed, pausing to feed Saaski the treat. "You know I'm talking about this stuff with Angelo and the FBI investigation. Don't be deliberately difficult. You're too smart for that and I would never buy it, so don't bother."

Mya stopped, aggravated that everyone had to talk about this topic when surely there were far more interesting things to consider in the world. Each patient she'd seen today had worn either a look of concern as if Angelo showing up was going to cause her to crack like an egg, or supportive anger, as if she needed their ire to bolster her own. By the end of the day, Mya's nerves were frayed and she just wanted to go home. But she wasn't about to let Iris know how deeply Angelo's presence affected her so she lied through her teeth.

"Honestly, it's just another day."

"*R-ii-ght,* because finding a dead body on the banks of the river and your ex-fiancé showing up to investigate are things that happen *all* the time. C'mon." Iris's mouth twisted sardonically, as if daring her to go there. "Try again."

She rubbed her eyes. "Okay, maybe not, but I meant it when I said Angelo being here doesn't affect me. I'm more than over him," she said, adding with a healthy dose of self-deprecation, "If I was still hung up on someone from fifteen years ago, I'd say I've got bigger problems."

"You're saying all the right things, but I know you. Angelo was a major part of your life and one that never gave you closure. Unresolved-love stuff is heavy, you know?"

Mya gave her friend a tired but wry expression. "Maybe for someone else. Like I said…I've moved on." Iris didn't seem convinced, but that was okay. Mya was more interested in getting home before some emergency called her back to the urgent care facility and completely ruined her plan for a long, uninterrupted soak

in the bathtub with a glass of red wine in her hand and
Moody Blues playing on the CD player.

"I still can't believe he's here," Iris said, as if Mya
hadn't spoken. "In fact, when I heard, I thought for
sure someone was pulling my leg, because why would
he even dare to come back here after all this time? It's
not like he has a lot of good memories or even family
to draw him home. Maybe if Waylon hadn't died..."

Mya nodded, trying to appear unaffected, but it was
difficult. Everyone on the reservation remembered that
awful day when Waylon was pulled from the river with
a bullet in his back and water in his lungs. He might
not have died if he hadn't fallen into the water. She'd
been with Angelo when he'd received the news. It had
been the worst shock of their lives. She couldn't blame
Angelo for wanting to leave, but he'd done more than
leave, he'd abandoned them all. Angelo had been next
in line to be hereditary chief, but he'd wanted nothing
to do with his heritage and had made that abundantly
clear when he'd split. She hitched a silent breath, trying
to shake off the grip of her current mood, blaming it on
fatigue.

"So...do you think you'll talk to Angelo while he's
here?"

Mya shot Iris a cool look. "Why should I?"

"You were engaged," Iris said simply, as if that carried any weight. "And crazy about each other. Like
stars-in-your-eyes-in-love kind of crazy. I think this
would be a golden opportunity to gain some closure."

"It was a long time ago," Mya reminded Iris with a
hint of the irritation beginning to boil over. It had been
fifteen years, she thought, gritting her teeth. *Get over it
already.* "Oh," she said, pretending she'd just remembered something important in the hopes of throwing

Iris off her current track. "Tomorrow we have the second shipment of flu shots coming in. They were on back order so we have a lot of people waiting for them. Maybe you could—"

Iris stopped Mya with a dark look. "Nice try. If you're so over Angelo why is your neck flushing?" Mya startled and her hand rose to her neck. Iris continued, "Listen, I'm worried about you. I hate to think that you're hurting and holding it all inside. You're right, fifteen years is a long time and it's time to close the book on Angelo Tucker, don't you think?"

"I closed the book the day he left," Mya said, her teeth gritting even as tears stung her eyes. She blinked them back, refusing to let them fall. Not here, not now. "But I certainly don't need everyone staring at me like I'm some kind of mental patient who's going to lose her mind at any given moment. Everyone is making it far worse than it truly is. Remember how you felt when everyone seemed to know your business after the attack?" Iris stiffened but nodded. "Well, it's just as uncomfortable for me. What I went through with Angelo was private and very painful. I don't need anyone telling me how to handle my business."

Iris took a moment to think over what Mya had said, and, when she nodded again, Mya knew she'd gotten through and relief followed. Of all the people on the reservation, Mya needed Iris solidly on her side, and that meant believing in her, too.

"Okay," Iris conceded, apology in her eyes. "I'm just trying to help."

"I know, but you don't need to worry. I'm over Angelo. I promise."

For the most part everything she was saying was true. Most days she could—and did—forget about Angelo.

But there were other days when she could almost hear his voice in her ear, promising always to be with her, and feel his touch on her body, igniting a firestorm along her sensitive nerve endings. It was far too easy to fall into the trap of nostalgia, but she could always rely on the pain that would follow to jerk her back to reality.

Angelo had done more than break her heart. He'd betrayed their people. That wasn't something she could forgive over a short, hey-how-you-been lunch date.

She grabbed her coat from her locker and slammed the door shut with perhaps more force than was necessary. "It doesn't matter to me if Angelo is here. My interest in his comings and goings died the day he ran like a coward."

Iris followed Mya as she exited the locker room, not quite ready to let it go, though she was considerably gentler in her approach. "I know there's a part of you that still cares, and that's okay to admit."

"What are you talking about?" Mya asked, not slowing her pace; if anything, she quickened it. "Angelo is part of my past, not my future. Should Sundance be worried about every old boyfriend you happen to run across?" she asked her friend pointedly, but Iris shrugged it off.

"If that's so," Iris continued, "why don't you give Porter a real chance? I know for a fact that he likes you a lot."

Porter Jacobs, a nice, endearingly straightforward man without a mean bone in his body…solid, dependable…nothing like Angelo. He didn't stand her up, he didn't have a temper, didn't harbor bitterness from his childhood—and he didn't make her heart race like Angelo once had. "What makes you think I haven't?"

she countered. The truth of the matter was that Porter had been slowly falling in love with her while Mya had simply been pleasantly enjoying his company. She had a feeling that if they continued along this vein, he'd pop the question, and she didn't know what she'd do. If she were smart she'd say yes, because Porter was an excellent catch and she'd be stupid to let him go. She bit back a guilty sigh. If only her feelings about Porter were as strong as his were for her. She returned to Iris, smiling sweetly as she approached her car. "Iris, honey, I love you, but drop it, all right? I don't care if Angelo is in town and I don't care why he's here. My association with that man ended a long time ago. As for Porter... I'm taking things slowly but that doesn't mean I'm not open to the possibility of something deeper."

Iris nodded and seemed to catch her drift well enough until Mya climbed into her car. "I'll bet Angelo is staying at his grandfather's," she said in a rush, just as Mya closed the door. Mya glared from behind the glass and Iris shrugged. "Not that you care...just saying. In case, you know, you change your mind."

Mya already knew where Angelo would be staying but she wasn't about to share that knowledge with Iris because her friend would read all sorts of nonsense into it. Mya huffed a short exasperated breath. She wasn't going to change her mind. She waved and drove away from the clinic.

Change her mind? Why should she? It's not like Angelo had.

Mya was nearly to her house when her cell phone jumped to life in her purse. She rummaged around in her bag, keeping her eyes on the twisty road, and pulled out the phone to check the caller ID. She grimaced, not because of who it was, but why he was calling.

"Hey, big brother," she answered, unable to hide the weariness in her tone. She didn't want a lecture or a warning that Angelo was in town. "What's up?"

"I have bad news and I have worse news. Which would you like first?" he asked, his voice grim. She could almost see the frown and unhappy scowl that were no doubt creasing his familiar face.

"Hmm, what choices...got any good news to cushion the delivery of the other two options?" she teased, hoping to lighten his mood, but no such luck. Sundance regarded his responsibility as a tribal police officer like a warrior—stoic and eyes-forward. She sighed. "All right, what's the bad news?"

"The bad news you already know—that no-good sack of garbage Angelo is on the rez—the worse news is I've heard that he might be in town longer than anticipated."

Mya chose to look past the insult to Angelo—she wasn't his champion—and focused on the second part. "Why? The coroner the FBI brought in already did the autopsy and the body is on its way off the reservation for burial."

"Angelo and his partner think that agent was here for more than fishing," he said.

Oh? She frowned. "Like what?"

"I don't know but they think it warrants a few extra days sniffing around."

"And how do you know this? Somehow I don't see Angelo sharing this information with you, of all people."

"He didn't," Sundance agreed gruffly. "But Porter told me that they went to the Tribal Center asking questions, checking if that agent had come around, and when someone mentioned that the agent had stopped by to gather a few pamphlets on the tribe's heritage, Porter overheard Angelo say to his partner that they'd have to stick around for a few days to try and find out what the agent had been looking for."

She withheld an unhappy sigh. Iris had been right, she wasn't totally unaffected by Angelo's presence and it would become harder to hide that fact the longer he stuck around. "Well, I doubt he'll find anything. The man was probably just enjoying a little fishing. Not everything is a big conspiracy. Sometimes people are just struck with plain bad luck."

"Listen, I talked with Angelo, made sure he knew I wouldn't just sit back and let him run all over you while he was here."

Mya reminded herself that Sundance was merely looking out for her and that his intentions were good, but fatigue was sapping her ability to keep her tone from becoming sharp. She was chafing at everyone's attempt to shield her from anything unpleasant as if she couldn't handle it. And where, pray tell, did everyone get this impression that she was weak and needed sheltering?

"Sonny," she said, using her childhood nickname for him, "I'm a grown woman and I'm fine. What happened between Angelo and me is such old history it doesn't hurt anymore," she lied. She wished it didn't hurt any longer. Maybe if the wound would finally heal, she could get on with her life. But as it was, she could only avoid direct contact with the raw pain in order to appear completely functioning. She'd become a pro at projecting a happy, healthy, well-adjusted facade— a fact she drew considerable comfort from. Only Iris suspected the truth. And maybe Sundance. She had to do her best to ease her brother's apprehension before he said or did something foolish. It wouldn't do to have her brother tangling with the FBI over an old tribal feud. "Listen, Angelo doesn't mean anything to me anymore and it doesn't matter that he's here. He's just a guy doing his job. That's all he is to me. The past is dead, Sonny," she assured him.

"That's what he said, too," Sundance admitted, causing her to stiffen a bit.

"He did?" she said, hating that Angelo's disinterest stung just a bit. It was good for her to move on, but knowing that Angelo had done the same didn't fill her with empowerment. No, actually it did the opposite.

She heard him exhale and she assumed it was from relief. "I worry about you," Sundance admitted. "I wish you'd just marry Porter. He's a good man."

Mya tensed without thought. If she heard one more person extolling Porter's virtues she'd scream. Yes, he was a good man. She was well aware of this, having dated him for nearly six months now, but she wasn't about to be pushed into marriage simply to relieve everyone else's irrational fear that the minute Angelo showed up again she'd forget about the last fifteen years and jump into bed with him. She tried not to be insulted but it rubbed her raw just the same. "Yes, well, I'm not ready to marry anyone and I'm sure Porter feels the same. I rather wish everyone would mind their own business."

"I know you're not some fragile piece of glass, Mya," Sundance acknowledged with a heavy sigh, mollifying her a little. "I know you're a highly capable woman. You take care of the entire tribe." *And yet...* She waited for him to continue. "I couldn't help myself. I see that man and I want to put my fist in his mouth."

Her ire faded and she smiled with a slight shake of her head. "You are a good brother and you always have been. But you don't have to worry. I can handle this. Truly."

"I believe you. I'll keep my mouth shut from here on out. I promise."

At that she laughed. "Don't make promises you can't keep, my brother. If I know the capacity of your heart to love, I also know the limits of your ability to control your mouth."

"Fine," he grumbled, totally caught. "Drive safely. I'll see you tomorrow."

She clicked off, her smile disappearing as her problem remained.

Angelo. How could one man cause such a stir?

Because Angelo had never been just one man.

As a kid, he'd been ridiculously beautiful with his fine-boned yet solid features, a benefit from his white Irish mother whose genetics had lent a caramel-mocha coloring to his Native American heritage while his Hoh father had given him proud cheekbones and straight white teeth. And things hadn't gone downhill the minute he hit puberty. An unwelcome shudder traveled through Mya, awakening sleeping parts of her that she would've preferred remain dormant.

"Damn it, Angelo…why couldn't you have stayed away?" she muttered, briefly giving in to the private anguish that she never shared. She wasn't the broken-hearted girl he'd left behind. But Mya couldn't deny that that broken-hearted girl was in there somewhere, because it was *her* hands that shook as she gripped the steering wheel and *her* stomach muscles that clenched against the quivering nervousness…not the Mya of today who was strong, confident, in control.

And, she noted almost desperately, at the moment, absent.

Chapter 6

Back in the car, Grace glanced over the pamphlets she'd grabbed while in the Tribal Center, which doubled as a visitors' bureau for wayward tourists. At one time, the tribe had made a good living on the salmon-fishing trade but the salmon numbers were no longer robust and they couldn't rely on fishing to sustain them.

"So, no casino, huh?" Grace said, reading over the literature while Angelo drove. "I thought all Indians got a casino, part of that government apology for wiping out the Native Americans with smallpox and whatnot."

Angelo gave Grace a short look, his mind on the case, not a history lesson, but when he saw true curiosity in her eyes, he relented, if only to get back to the case. "There's not much room for a casino on a reservation only a square mile long," he said. "So, no, not every tribe gets a casino."

"Bummer." Grace continued perusing the paper. "So what's this I hear that you're some chief or something?"

He started, unable to disguise the internal shock of her discovery. She arched an eyebrow as if to say *What's that all about?* and waited for his answer. "I don't want to talk about it," he said, taking great care not to grit his teeth. "It's stupid, means nothing, and has no bearing on the case."

She shrugged. "Maybe so, but, I don't know, sounds like a big deal. Does this mean you're a prince of your tribe or something?"

"No. Drop it."

"Touchy. Can't fault a girl for being curious. It's not something you hear every day."

"Yeah, well, it's not something I like to talk about. There's hard feelings on both sides," he said, keeping his eyes on the road.

Silence laden with curiosity on Grace's part filled the car. He wished Grace hadn't caught that little tidbit about his life, but, of all people, he trusted Grace the most. Still, he hated talking about it, because when the subject was brought up, he was forced to acknowledge how royally he'd screwed up. Knowing Grace would follow his lead, he brought the case back to the forefront. "I think tomorrow we may need to pay a visit to the wife. I've had Hicks's financials emailed to me. We can spend the rest of the afternoon going through them to see if anything stands out. I want to get a better sense of the man."

"Why? We already have the wife's statement," Grace said, frowning.

"Because obviously something was missed. I want to talk to the woman myself. The key is staring us right in the face. I can feel it."

"Is that your Indian mojo talking?" Grace joked, but he wasn't laughing.

"No. It's called solid investigative work," he said, not quite able to keep the sharpness from his tone, which he immediately regretted.

Grace dropped the jocularity, catching the not-so-subtle hint that he didn't find any humor in the situation and her mouth firmed in a thin line. "Hicks lived in Beaver, Washington. It's about forty-five minutes from here. Listen, I can handle a grouch. I didn't spend two tours in the army without leaving with a thick skin, but I'm not in the army any longer and I don't take kindly to being snapped at for asking the obvious questions."

She was right. He was being a jerk. "I'm not used to people knowing my business and that's all I get here. You can't sneeze around here without someone hearing about it on the other side of the reservation. It makes me twitchy." Not to mention, he'd forgotten what it felt like to be judged every minute of the day. It created a pressure in his chest, as if an elephant had planted its butt right on his sternum, and he didn't like it.

"All right," she allowed, accepting his attempt at an apology. That was the great thing about Grace, she wasn't like a lot of women who dealt in emotional currency. She was blunt and when she had a point to make, she didn't beat around the bush. "Sorry if I was trespassing. We've all got skeletons, I suppose."

Amen to that. "It's hard being here," he admitted. "My whole family is buried in this soil." And then there was Mya to contend with. Not so much a skeleton but a living, breathing reminder of what a coward he was. "Can we get back to the case now?" he asked, almost begging.

"Do you have cell service at your place?" she asked.

"Something tells me there's no coffee shack with free Wi-Fi anywhere around here."

"You got that right, and yeah, I've got service. I checked last night before going to bed," he said, silently thanking Grace for knowing that he'd begun to squirm talking about his past. He blinked the grit from his eyes, a reminder that he'd slept poorly the night before.

"The town of Beaver isn't much to look at, just a spot in the road, really. I used to drive there to get away from the reservation," he shared, almost as a bone thrown to Grace for shutting her out so completely earlier.

He remembered Beaver from a youth spent anywhere but the reservation. He'd told Mya he just liked to drive, using the excuse to spend time alone together, but the real reason was that the reservation was a weight on his shoulders he didn't want and his grandfather knew it. The knowledge hadn't sat well with Papa though Angelo knew Papa had been hoping that with maturity would come acceptance. But then Waylon died, and Angelo had known his path was elsewhere.

The fact of the matter was, Waylon should have been the next chief. His soul had been grounded in Hoh soil. He'd loved the stories, felt the pride of his heritage and would have gladly sat at the head of the Tribal Council without complaint.

A hollow ache rang in his chest for the loss of his little brother, reminding him how empty he'd felt since that day. Now all he had was his work. And that had to be enough.

Mya tried to give her full attention to Porter. Guilt at putting him off several times this week had prompted her to accept his lunch invitation, but her thoughts kept wandering to Angelo and his investigation. She told herself her curiosity was only based on the fact that a homicide on the reservation was rare and she hoped he found answers quickly. But that would be dishonest, and she was too smart to play such mind games with herself. Still, it wasn't fair to Porter, so she refocused in the hopes that he hadn't noticed she'd checked out for a minute or two.

No such luck.

"You're a million miles away today," Porter teased, reaching across the table to touch her hand.

She resisted the urge to pull away and instead forced a smile. "I'm sorry. Patients are on my mind, I guess," she said, offering a white lie in deference to Porter's feelings and ignoring the bigger twinge of guilt that followed. "So I hear you're going to participate in the Tribal Canoe Journey this year?" she asked, being polite.

His smile widened as he said, "I have room on my canoe for one more if you'd like to come along."

"Oh," she said, briefly entertaining the idea. The Tribal Canoe Journey was a yearly event celebrated by multiple tribes to promote cultural, spiritual and personal growth. She'd never actually been on a canoe team before and the idea appealed to her, but her schedule didn't allow for much wiggle room so she'd never volunteered. "I'll think about it. How about I let you know?"

"You've got plenty of time," Porter said. "The event isn't until July, so no rush."

Their lunch arrived and Mya gratefully turned her attention to her salad. Why she felt riddled with guilt she had no idea, but it made sitting here with Porter an excruciating ordeal rather than an enjoyable experience.

"So, the reservation is experiencing a bit of excitement, what with the big guns coming in to investigate that homicide," Porter said, taking a bite of his sandwich. "Have you managed to pick up any details? I know the clinic is the information hub around here," he teased, but she heard a note of seriousness beneath the light joke.

Damn. She'd hoped to get through lunch without having to bring up Angelo or the investigation. A discussion would only stir up questions, and she wasn't ready to answer any that involved Angelo. She shrugged. "I don't know more than anyone else. A man was found shot and he turned out to be an FBI agent. I'm sure it'll all blow over quickly enough. Sad about the man, though. I feel bad for his wife."

"How do you know he was married?"

Damn it. She knew because of Angelo. "Sundance told me," she fibbed, cringing at how easily the lies were flowing from her mouth at the moment. She never lied to Porter and the fact that she was starting now because of Angelo only served to further ruin any hope she'd held of enjoying her lunch.

Porter stilled when her fidgeting fingers drew attention to her discordant thoughts. She withdrew her hands from the table but it was too late.

"What's wrong?" he asked. "Something is bothering you."

She risked a short smile. "It's nothing," she said, but Porter wasn't buying it. He pulled away, his handsome face somber, his eyes troubled.

"I know you and Angelo Tucker have a history. Everyone on the reservation knows that. But I didn't want to be like everyone else and assume that it's a problem for you. Was I wrong in my assumption that the past is the past?"

She almost scoffed at his question—the very fact

that he'd asked irritated her—but he, of all people, had cause to wonder. She wanted to reassure him unreservedly, but there was an infinitesimal part of her that prevented her from giving him the assurances he needed. Her hesitation caused the corners of his mouth to turn down. He swore lightly under his breath.

"The past *is* the past," Mya said, in an almost desperate bid to patch what she'd just punched a hole through. "I'm totally over him. It's just hard for me to have him here after all this time." Perhaps if she kept telling herself that, it would become true. "I care for you deeply, Porter. Trust in that."

His frown intensified, her words having the opposite effect. "You care deeply for me? We've been dating for six months. I was hoping for a bit more," he said, bitterness leaching into his tone.

She couldn't give what she didn't feel. And she knew she wasn't in love with Porter. But maybe with more time...

"Porter, let's table this conversation for a later date," she said quietly, hating how their luncheon had been ruined.

"Later when?" he inquired, his solicitous tone betraying a level of sarcasm that was hard to ignore. "I suspect this is a conversation we should've had a long time ago."

"Why? I was happy with our arrangement," she said stiffly. "But I sense that's not the way you feel."

"No. It's not. I was hoping things were moving in a different direction."

She plucked at her napkin under the table, wishing she wasn't having this conversation, but how could she blame him? He needed honesty and she ought to give it him. She heard her brother's advice in her head, chastising her for not giving Porter a chance, but she couldn't get her lips to move. Wouldn't it be a simple—and smart—thing to give Porter what he needed? He was a good man, solid and dependable. He'd be a good father if they chose to have children and he respected their heritage. But for all those admirable qualities, she knew with a certainty that she couldn't tie herself to him permanently. Her eyes watered and her mouth worked soundlessly, searching for the words but she needn't have bothered. Porter's expression fell and his gaze dropped to his plate where his half-eaten sandwich remained. "Let's finish up so I can take you back to the clinic. I've lost my appetite."

"Porter—"

He held up his hand, stopping her, his voice pained. "Don't."

Her mouth tightened but she nodded in understanding, her food sitting like a lump of lead in her stomach.

Fresh anger at Angelo washed over her in a wave. Even fifteen years later the man was still messing with her life. She followed Porter out and on the silent ride back to the clinic she cursed Angelo for returning, but mostly she cursed herself for not being able to move on.

Angelo and Grace returned to his grandfather's place and, after setting up a portable printer to the laptop, spent the afternoon combing through pages of Byron Hicks's personal life as it was laid out in the form of his financial transactions.

"I always feel bad for the sorry sap whenever I have to go through their bank accounts," Grace admitted, leaning back to stretch after an hour of silent busywork. "Makes me wonder what someone would think of me if they discovered I spent way too much money on antique tea sets. I mean, you can get a snapshot of a person's habits but it only tells a fraction of the story."

Angelo looked up. "Really? Tea sets?"

She shrugged defensively. "They remind me of my old aunt who lived in San Francisco in one of those big Victorians. She was nice to me. I have good memories. But you see, that's what I mean. Unless someone knew me, they'd never understand why a person like me would collect something like that."

Angelo chuckled. "I doubt someone would look twice at your penchant for collecting tea sets. I'd worry more about your cholesterol, seeing as you eat out more than anyone I know. Do you even know how to boil water?"

"I can rip open an MRE pretty handily," Grace quipped with good humor. "Speaking of, I brought a few in case we got caught without a place to grab some grub. You want one? I have meatloaf with gravy or spaghetti with meat sauce."

"As tempting as that offer is, I think I'll pass. You know, most people stop eating those things when they no longer have to."

"I like them. They're fast, easy and nutritionally adequate. Plus, the cleanup is easy. What's not to like?"

"Flavor?"

"Don't knock it 'til you try it. You might be surprised."

"I'm not hungry enough to brave the MRE. Thanks but no thanks."

"Suit yourself. I think I'll have the spaghetti. Be right back," she said and hopped from her chair to go to the car.

Angelo returned to his papers, scanning and taking notes. He was starting on the third month of Hicks's bank statement when his gaze snagged on something.

He leaned forward and highlighted the charge, looking for similar charges.

Grace returned with a brown-packaged MRE in hand. She started to say something but then noted his body language. "You found something?" she asked, meal forgotten.

"Maybe." He handed her a sheaf of papers. "A withdrawal of $300 and then a subsequent cash deposit of $1,000. A month or so later I found a similar withdrawal and a deposit of $700. But the next month he had two withdrawals of $500 and no deposits."

"What are you thinking?" Grace asked, grabbing her highlighter and beginning to scan. "Gambling?"

"Looks like it. Do we have his credit card receipts?" he asked, flagging another suspicious withdrawal.

Grace stopped and fished through her papers. "Yeah, right here."

"Check those, too," he instructed. "A man with something to prove might harbor a need for other types of validation. If I were taking a guess, I'd say Byron wasn't much of a successful gambler, judging by these withdrawals and the subsequent deposits. They certainly don't match."

They spent another four hours gleaning figures in the hope of putting together a profile of a dead man. Finally, they finished the task and both were ready to grind their eyeballs out from the strain, but they'd managed to tally up a year's worth of withdrawals totaling approximately $25,000.

"That's a lot of coin," Grace said at the end, amazed and disgusted at the same time. He and Grace shared a low opinion of gamblers and neither saw the point of throwing away good money. "So do you think we have a man with a gambling addiction?"

"That's what it looks like. Plenty of places to choose from with twenty-seven casinos in the state of Washington."

"And your tribe had the colossal bad luck to put down roots in this square mile of nothing. Man, I bet you're wishing your ancestors had been more discerning in their selection of the real estate," Grace said dryly amid a yawn.

He grunted in answer, then grabbed a map, marking each Indian casino in the state. "The closest casinos to the area are in Neah Bay, Port Angeles and Sequim. My guess is Neah Bay."

"So, going by the numbers we see here, he was in debt," Grace surmised.

"Yeah, and people who are in debt up to their eyeballs usually do dumb stuff like borrow money from less-than-legit enterprises."

"You think this was a hit because he owed money? I don't know, loan sharks don't usually kill the people who owe them money, makes it hard to get paid. They prefer to threaten the person's loved ones or even chop off a finger."

"Does that happen anywhere but the movies?" he asked. "I've never worked any cases like that before. You don't see too much of it around this area, not like Vegas, I suppose."

"I've seen it in a few cases, not here but in New York, sure. You tangle with the wrong person, you're going to pay one way or another. But with all these Indian casinos springing up all over the place, I bet you start seeing more of that kind of element hanging around. Like moths to a flame."

He could follow her logic, prompting him to suggest a road trip. "We could take a drive up to Neah Bay and check it out, see if any of the local players remember Hicks," he said, cracking a yawn himself. "It's the best lead we've had to go on since Hicks ended up dead."

"Might as well." Grace tossed her highlighter to the table and swung her leg over the chair seat as she stood with a long stretch. "My back feels permanently kinked. I'm hitting the sack. How about you?"

He didn't relish another night tossing and turning, his dreams veering too close to Mya for true restful sleep, but exhaustion was starting to take its toll. The numbers were blurring before him anyway. "Yeah," he finally agreed, rising and silently cursing the hard chair he'd been sitting on for the past three hours without a break. His papa had been a simple man with simple tastes. The chairs were Mission-style with only the padding of his rear to cushion his bones. And he was feeling it. He tried not to hobble. A man had his pride.

He needed to crash, but first he had to throw some food down his gullet. His stomach felt ready to digest itself. Grace chuckled and pointed to the remaining MRE on the counter in the kitchen. "Bon appétit."

"Good God, have mercy," he murmured with a healthy dose of apprehension, but he was starved and he hadn't had the foresight to stop by the market before heading to his grandfather's place. He opened the MRE and waited for the internal heater to do its thing, then stared at the food with a jaundiced eye.

"Don't be such a puss. It's good for you. Tastes better than nothing."

"Remind me to hit the store tomorrow," he said, right before shoveling a bite of the meatloaf with its brown gravy into his mouth. He chewed slowly. Eh, it wasn't terrible. He took another bite and actually smiled around the hot stuff in his mouth. "My grandfather probably would've loved these things. He was proficient at a very small list of dinner items, most of which involved some kind of fish he hauled from the river. We ate a lot of crawdads," he admitted.

Grace stared at him with the kind of deep speculation that usually made people nervous and said, "We've worked together for three years and in one trip I've realized I don't know much about you. This whole chief thing is interesting, whether you believe it or not. I wish I had something so unique in my personal history. The most interesting thing in my family tree is that I'm a distant cousin to the inventor of the hula hoop."

He did a double take. "Really?"

"Yeah. So my mother says, but it's not like it's a real claim to fame, you know?"

"Neither is mine." Angelo sighed and then shrugged. "It's a simple and meaningless title. I don't even get a good parking pass to anywhere," he said, trying for lightness in his tone, but the lead in his stomach—or maybe that was the meatloaf—caused him to fail. He crumpled the wrapping from his MRE and tossed it in the trash.

"The Queen of England has a meaningless title too but she's still pretty cool."

"Not even the same," he said, though Grace's attempt at a parallel at the very least made him smile.

Grace grinned, but then sobered. "So, is that doc an Indian princess or something?"

"Mya? No. It doesn't work that way." Not that she didn't have the regal bearing of a proud warrior princess, he thought with a smidge of pride he had no right to feel. He cleared his throat, saying in a tone that conveyed he was too tired to have this conversation, "We hit the road at 0700."

"All right. I get it. Too painful. I know I ought to stop digging around, but I can't seem to help myself. You're a mystery man, Tucker," she said with a wink before tucking herself into her bedroll, her shoes once again lined up neatly within easy grabbing distance. If there was ever a catastrophic disaster and the world devolved into the most primitive and aggressive behavior, he wanted Grace by his side. She was a smart investigator, but deep down she remained a soldier. He found that quality comforting. At least he knew what to expect with Grace.

Not so with Mya.

Damn, why'd he have to let his mind go there? The fatigue must've weakened his ability to stay focused. He'd told himself he wasn't going to think about Mya tonight. And up until this moment, lying alone in his cold bed, he'd succeeded.

Over the years, he'd often thought of calling Mya, but when he'd played out the scenario in his head he couldn't seem to find a favorable ending. The worst one in his imagination had Mya pulling out a shotgun and blowing a hole in his chest. Granted, that nightmare had been after a particularly morose drinking binge, but the image had stuck in his mind. After the way he'd left her, he supposed he deserved a bullet somewhere non-lethal but highly painful, like a kneecap or elbow. Of course, now there was too much animosity to drop by casually and say, "Hey, Mya, it's been a long time... how've you been?"

It's not like they could pretend the past didn't happen—as evidenced by the stiff and brittle encounters they'd shared recently.

Was she dating? Married? He hadn't seen a ring,

not that he'd looked specifically, but he supposed he'd remember that detail if she were wearing one.

He rolled to his side and plumped the pillow into some semblance of comfort but it remained flat as an old, deflated inner tube and nearly as uncomfortable. "Mya," he breathed on a soft sigh, wondering if she had a clue how seeing her again had thrown his carefully ordered world into chaos. Sure, he played it off well—it was his job to seem implacable—but he knew the truth of it. Mya made his insides a mess.

Get it together, he chastised himself, annoyed that he was wallowing in some strange nostalgic mindset. *This too shall pass...God, please let it pass.*

This kind of melancholy could drive a man to do something crazy.

Chapter 7

The drive to the Neah Bay casino was accompanied by a pounding rain that could soak a person within minutes if they stayed out in it. It didn't serve to endear the area to Grace, and by the time they arrived at the casino her mutinous scowl seemed permanently etched onto her face.

They scrambled from the car to the front doors, handing the keys to the valet, and headed inside.

The perfect lighting, geared to make people want to stay and spend more money, filled the expansive slot room, and the sound of clanging, dinging and other racket was an assault to the ears. They went straight for the pit boss, knowing he or she would likely recognize Byron's picture if he was winning or losing with any sort of regularity. A flash of their badges and the pit boss was friendly, amenable and ready to help; Angelo got the distinct impression that it was an act purely for their benefit.

"We have reason to believe this man frequented your establishment, losing a significant amount of money over the past year. He might've last been seen here a month ago," Grace said, referencing the date of Hicks's last cash withdrawal.

The pit boss, a woman with sharp eyes and a wide smile, accepted the photo and studied it without a flicker in her brown eyes. She returned the photo with a shake of her head. "We see a lot of people. It's impossible to remember one man," she said.

"This man is dead. Try a little harder to remember," Grace said, thrusting the photo back at the woman, who reacted with a trace of irritation but otherwise did as Grace instructed. This time her memory seemed improved as she gestured toward one particular blackjack table.

"He appeared to enjoy Carolina's table," she said. "But he had a run of bad luck and expended his line of credit. So you say he's deceased?" she inquired, the picture of solicitousness. "How unfortunate."

"May we talk with Carolina?" Angelo asked.

"Of course." She smiled. "This way."

She led them to a pretty woman who looked to be in her mid-twenties and introduced them.

"Carolina, Special Agents Tucker and Kelly would like to ask you some questions about a patron who tragically died recently. Please give them your utmost cooperation." With that and a nod of understanding between them, she left them with the dealer.

"He's dead?" she asked, looking distressed.

"Yes," Angelo said, watching her carefully. He imagined she had a lot of straight men who flocked to her table. Being opposite a pretty woman made losing a bit more palatable for some men. "He seemed to like your table, according to the pit boss."

She nodded, almost guiltily. "He was nice. But a very bad blackjack player."

He and Grace exchanged looks. "Your pit boss said his line of credit at the casino had been exhausted. Do you know of anyone around here who might be in the business of extending credit for those who run into those kinds of situations?"

"No, not that I know of," Carolina said, but her eyes betrayed her and Grace pounced.

"We both know that there's a lucrative side business for dealers who provide these types of people with contacts."

She stiffened. "I'd never do that."

"It's hard to make an honest living these days. No one would fault you for needing a little something on the side," Angelo countered with understanding, playing the good cop. She looked young, vulnerable, afraid of losing her job. "Listen, we're not interested in you. We just need to find out what might have happened to our fellow agent."

Carolina chewed her lip, visibly caught between spilling her guts and retreating for cover, but in the end, her conscience must've gotten the better of her because she started talking quickly and in a hushed tone. "Okay, I don't know much but there is a guy who seems to provide a *service* to people who've shown a need for a little extra cash."

"What's this person's name?" Grace asked.

"Well, he's known as Mr. C, but I don't actually know his name. Listen, this information didn't come from me, okay? I've got kids at home who depend on me. If Mr. C finds out that it was me who gave him up, he'll…"

"Is he violent? Has he threatened people before?" Angelo asked.

She offered a nervous shrug. "Well, he's not a nice guy. People have said things…but I don't know if they're true. They might just be rumors, but I don't want to be the one to test whether they're real."

"We don't give up our sources. Where can we find this Mr. C?"

"You don't find him, he finds you."

Angelo wasn't buying that. "How'd Byron Hicks get a hold of him?"

"I don't know," she said. "Look, are we done here? I can't spend all day talking to you two. No offense, but time is money, and besides, if Mr. C's people see me talking to you they'll know it was me, so please leave my station and go talk to someone else."

Angelo motioned to Grace and they moved on, leaving Carolina alone as she'd asked. Once out of earshot, he said, "So, aside from the dealers, where else would a loan shark sniff around for desperate gamblers in need of more coin?"

"The business office, I'd wager," she replied with a nod. "Let's ask around."

They made their rounds to the other tables but, as they'd expected, came up empty, which was okay. They'd gotten what they needed from Carolina and didn't want to put her in any danger. They found the business office and, after flashing their credentials, noticed one of the clerks trying to silently slip out the side door. Angelo hauled the man back inside and shoved him against the wall while Grace cleared the room so they could handle this in private. "Leaving so soon? We haven't even said our hellos yet," he said.

The man's eyes were twitchy, his skin clammy. Angelo grimaced and wiped his hand on his trousers. He stepped closer and peered into the man's face. Then his lip curled. "Meth head," he announced. "You're high as a kite, aren't you?" It was a rhetorical question. He could tell without having to put his finger on the man's pulse that it was kicking faster than normal. "When was the last time you used?" he asked.

"I—I don't use drugs," he tried bluffing, but Angelo didn't have time for the bullshit. He was interested in bigger fish.

"Don't waste my time. Who's Mr. C? I'm guessing you feed Mr. C the tips on who's hard-up for cash and likely to cave to his offer of a loan."

"I don't know what you're talking about," the man said, crossing his arms and trying to look defiant when in fact, he looked ready to wet himself.

Angelo glanced at Grace. "I think we might have a terrorist threat, don't you?"

"Yes, I believe this man may be a threat to national security. I suppose we ought to haul him in and give him a standard AC1 interrogation."

"AC1? What's that mean? I'm no terrorist," he protested, as he continued to slide his tongue over chapped lips. "You can't do this...this is a sovereign nation... you've got no power here."

"A threat to America supersedes all. You can thank the Patriot Act for that." Angelo smiled and it caused the man to quail a little. And just because he was annoyed at the piece of scum for trying to bluff him, he poured it on a little thick in the hopes that the drug addict would start to babble. "I think the strip search is the worst part, but then again, the waterboarding isn't a cakewalk, either."

"Oh, yeah," Grace agreed, shaking her head. "When it comes to terrorists, it's as if the Geneva Convention was never enacted. It's like carte blanche. Frankly, the stuff they do as standard protocol in an AC1 turns my stomach, and I've served two tours in the U.S. military on foreign soil."

"But I'm not a terrorist," the meth addict exclaimed as a rivulet of sweat slid down his cheek.

"Says who?" Grace's congenial manner slipped away and there was nothing kind or soft in her demeanor. "You tell us what we want to know or we'll see to it that your insides are turned upside down and backward until you won't know if you're supposed to piss or spit. You think your biggest problem is saving your butt from getting canned? Or protecting this loan shark, Mr. C? Oh no, let me educate you. Those will be the least of your worries once the U.S. Government gets a hold of your sweating, meth-soaked ass. And the best part? It's all legal. Well, most of it. Now talk, I'm losing patience and I'm hungry."

"I—I have a phone number that I call when I've got someone who fits the criteria," he said, shaking so much his words were running together.

"What's his real name?"

"I don't know. All's I got is a number."

Grace looked to Angelo, who shrugged. "Guess it'll do." He stared at the man. "Call him. Tell him you have a winner. I want to have a chat with the man."

The man pulled his cell phone from his pocket and speed-dialed a contact. "I've got a juicy one, dumb and glum," he said into the phone, then hung up. Obviously the statement was some kind of code.

"Now we wait. How long does it usually take?" Angelo asked.

"Not long. A few minutes or so."

"Damn, not enough time to grab a sandwich," Grace grumbled, seemingly forgetting about the meth head until he tried slinking away. She slapped her palm against the wall by his head and he jumped. "Going somewhere? We'll need you for introductions. What's your name anyway?"

He swallowed. "Gage."

"Well, Gage—nice name by the way—we're going to need you to set us up with your friend Mr. C. Think you can do that?" Grace asked but didn't wait for an answer. "Okay, great. Thanks. You're a doll."

"He'll kill me," Gage pleaded, begging even. "Don't make me do this."

"Where do you usually send his prospective *clients?*" Angelo asked.

"They meet at the bar. I always put them on the second stool nearest to the bathroom. And then he takes it from there."

"Classy. What do you get out of it?" Grace asked.

"A small bump."

"Which is?" Grace prompted.

"Ten percent of whatever he's borrowing."

"How much did you make off Byron Hicks?"

"Who?"

Angelo growled. "The federal agent whose death we're investigating."

"Oh man, I didn't have nothing to do with that. I don't remember how much I made. My brain isn't working great. You've got me all freaked out," Gage complained with a whine that grated on Angelo's ears. He gestured to Grace who let up the pressure, moving away from the man before he wet himself. "Is that all you want?"

"Yeah, get out of here. But if I find out that you've tipped him off I'll come find you," Grace promised, eliciting a jerky nod of understanding from Gage before he scuttled away from them. "You want to be the client or do you want me to?"

"I'll take it. You can come rescue me. I know how you love being the hero," he said dryly, causing Grace to cackle in laughter.

"That I do."

Within ten minutes, a man stepped up to the bar and ordered a cocktail, taking his time before saying to Angelo, who appeared to be nursing a beer, "I heard you were down on your luck."

Angelo smirked, then turned to the man, gauging him to be in his late forties, saying, "Actually, I think my luck just changed. Special Agent Angelo Tucker." He flashed his badge and the man moved as if to walk away, but Grace peeled away from the wall where she'd been stationed and boxed him in. "As I was saying, my name is Special Agent Tucker...I have a few questions for you. What's your name?"

"Howard Odgerson," he said warily, settling back on his stool. "What can I do for you, Agent Tucker?"

"Well, for one, you can tell me if you recognize this man." He produced Hicks's picture and placed it on the bar. "And two, you can tell me if you provided him with a loan."

"I don't know what you're talking about," Odgerson said. "And I don't know the man."

"Grace?" Angelo motioned and she produced a handheld fingerprint machine. "This will just take a minute. Place your index finger on the flat spot, please."

"Why?"

"To take your fingerprint. That much should be obvious."

"Am I under arrest?"

"Nope. Just need to make sure you are who you say you are, Howie," Angelo said, deliberately baiting him. If he was shady he wouldn't want to put his finger on that machine. Chances were his name wasn't Howard, either. Angelo was also willing to bet that whoever he truly was, he was logged in the system. "But we're investigating a murder and right now we find you of interest. Word has it you're in the business of providing funds to poor saps who can't seem to find it through regular channels."

"Who told you that?" Howard asked, shifting his gaze away from the machine, plainly uncomfortable.

"Never mind the who. Did you know this man?"

"I said no."

"Look again," Angelo suggested in a tone that told the man it wasn't an option to refuse.

Howard reluctantly grabbed the photo and peered at it more closely. After a long moment, he shrugged and shook his head. "No. I don't recognize the man. I've never done business with him."

"Why don't I believe you?" Angelo asked, nodding to Grace who moved forward and thrust the machine toward Howard. "Your finger, please."

"I got rights," Howard said, sweat starting to bead on his upper lip.

"And I don't have patience. Either give up what you know or put your damn finger on that machine and we'll play match the felon to the identity. Trust me, in that game, I win."

Howard muttered an expletive under his breath and

glowered at both Grace and Angelo but finally relented. "All right, I gave him some cash, but he already paid the debt."

"So why didn't you just say that up front?" Grace asked.

"That's my business, not yours," he snapped, which Grace didn't appreciate at all. Her expression hardened and he realized he must've screwed with the wrong agent. "Listen, I run a legitimate business—"

"There's a reason *loan shark* isn't something you put on the résumé. It's not legit," Angelo countered, yet he was troubled by the dead end. "So, he paid in full?"

"Yeah." Howard nodded. "Surprised me, too. Here I thought the guy was a good lead and then he up and paid off the debt with minimal interest factored in."

He and Grace shared a look of disappointment. Howie might be scum preying on gambling addicts, but he wasn't their guy—at least not today.

"Keep your nose clean, Howie. We're watching you," Angelo said as Grace pocketed her machine. "And I might think of getting out of the loan-shark business if you want to stay out of prison. Mr. C is closing up shop in this place. Understand?"

"Or what?" he dared to ask.

Grace stepped up with a hard-edged smile. "Or else you and I get to know each other real well. And I'm not a nice, gentle kind of person."

"She's crazy," Howard said, not quite sure what to make of Grace's threat, but the uncertainty in his stare told Angelo he took her seriously.

Angelo grinned. "You have no idea. It's what I like about her."

They cleared the casino doors and when the valet brought the car around, Grace's low rumble of laughter followed his incredulous, "AC1? What the hell does that mean? Nice touch."

"She's crazy," Grace mimicked with a grin. "That's fun. We should terrorize scum buckets more often. It's a great stress reliever."

He laughed but sobered quickly when he realized they'd hit a dead end. "You know this means we're back to square one," he said.

Grace's mirth faded away as she sighed. "Yeah. I was hoping to find more to go on with the gambling angle but now it seems not only was Hicks a boring individual in life, he was fairly boring in death, too."

"That's harsh," he said.

Grace shrugged. "I know. Just calling it like I see it. So now what?"

"Back to the wife. Something was definitely missed."

Chapter 8

Angelo and Grace stepped to the front door of Byron Hicks's house and while Grace knocked, Angelo took in his surroundings. The place was moderately sized, not new, but in decent shape. No neighbors close by, the trees provided a canopy of privacy that was common to the area, but it was a generally "nice" stretch of property. It was as bland as Hicks's personnel file, thought Angelo.

The door opened and a short, stout, blonde woman peered at them with red-rimmed eyes. She surmised they were agents by their garb, which didn't surprise Angelo given her husband's employment. "I already gave a statement," she said, sniffing and wiping at her nose with a tissue. "And an agent already picked up his issue effects."

"We're sorry to bother you again, Mrs. Hicks," Angelo said with the gravity the situation required. "But we have some additional questions regarding your husband's fishing trip to the Hoh reservation."

At the mention of the reservation her mouth trembled and turned down with obvious disgust. "I told him to drop it. It was none of his business but he wouldn't listen. That was so like Byron—filled with delusions of grandeur—chasing after a story that'd been long dead and no one cared about."

Angelo's ears pricked at the careless clue dropped at their feet and his previous questions about the gambling went stone-cold. "What story? According to your statement, your husband went to the Hoh to fish salmon."

"And apparently to gamble at nearby casinos," Grace murmured, unaware of how the woman's unknowing comment had affected him.

At the mention of the gambling, the wife's cheeks flushed and she started to say something, but Angelo cut her off, uninterested in that aspect of the man's life. At this point he couldn't care less if Hicks had mortgaged the family home to fund his gambling escapades; Angelo wanted to know what the wife meant. "What story? What was your husband working on that no one knew about?"

Her eyes widened as if she'd just realized her mistake but extreme grief and bitterness at her loss ate away at her ability to maintain any semblance of caution, which worked for Angelo perfectly. She wiped at her nose again and gestured for them to follow. He and Grace exchanged looks of interest and stepped over the threshold.

The woman sank into a recliner that was ringed with soiled tissues. After grabbing two fresh tissues, she began with a watery sigh. "I don't know why I didn't just come out and admit it when the Bureau asked for my statement…I guess it was force of habit. Byron didn't want anyone to know what he was digging into. He was paranoid that someone else might come along and take the case from him before he had the chance to crack it…but honestly, at this point, what does it matter? He's dead because of it and I don't rightly care. I'm…a…" her eyes welled and she pressed the tissue to her face to catch the tears as they spilled down her cheeks "…widow now. And it's not fair."

Angelo felt a modicum of sympathy for Mrs. Hicks, but his eagerness for information overrode all else. "Go on," he said, earning a look that said *Dial it down a notch* from Grace. "Take your time," he tacked on for appearance's sake, when, in reality, he wanted to shake her and say *Get on with it, woman.*

"He was a good agent," Grace said to the woman, encouraging her to continue. "Tell us what he was working on. Maybe we can find out who did this."

The woman shrugged, her gaze darting, as if she were unsure what to share and what to hold back. Angelo jumped in, pressing. "I know you want justice for your husband. We're on your side. He was a fellow agent and we don't take his death lightly. Someone needs to pay. We can't make sure that they do without your help. You have to be his voice," he said, holding her stare with his own. He could feel her wavering. He just needed a little more pressure and she'd crack. "If you know something, it's your duty to tell us, but forget all that…do it for Byron."

Her breath hitched in her throat and her eyes welled. "It was a cold case," she shared, her voice small and grief-stricken. "Something about a kid who was killed on the reservation more than fifteen years ago."

Cold shock washed over him. Only one kid had been

killed on the reservation, and the culprit never found. His throat tightened as if someone had wrapped their fingers around it and squeezed. "Go on," he said, his nerves tensing.

The woman dabbed at her eyes. "I don't know a lot," she said apologetically. "Byron didn't like to share too much about his work. He said it was against protocol to share details about cases and I respected that so I didn't ask too many questions. But he was so worked up about this case and I never understood why. I mean I felt bad for the kid—he was only sixteen when he died—but really, it wasn't our problem and I didn't know why he cared so much."

"What was the name of the kid?" Grace asked, shooting Angelo a dark look. "Do you remember that?"

She nodded, shrinking a little from the intense stare Angelo was giving her. "I told him to drop it," she said defensively. "I knew it was going to be nothing but trouble—"

"The name," Angelo cut in, barely able to breathe. "What was the name?"

"Waylon Tucker," she answered in a small voice, glancing at Grace for help. "He was sure that if he broke the cold case he'd be promoted and then we could afford to leave Beaver and move closer to Seattle. But I told him to leave it be. He didn't listen," she added mournfully. "And now I'm a widow."

"Why that case?" Angelo asked, surprised his voice didn't waver.

"Well, he came across the case when he started going up there to fish and once he started poking around, he was hooked. It gave him a thrill, I think, to be doing something that mattered. He was always being passed over for promotions and he wanted to prove that he could be a good investigator."

"That case wasn't FBI jurisdiction," Angelo said, mostly to Grace. He returned to the woman. "Did he mention any contacts he'd made while on the case?"

She shook her head. "But he seemed excited about something he'd found, which was why he wanted to spend more time on the reservation. He wasted a week's worth of vacation that we were going to use to go to see my mother in Utah, spending it chasing after ghosts."

More specifically, the ghost of Angelo's little brother.

He needed air. He mumbled something that sounded like his thanks and then bolted for the door. Once outside, he drew a deep lungful of cold air, his hands bracketing his hips as he fought for clarity of mind, but Waylon as he'd last seen him kept battering his calm.

Sixteen was too young to die. Some coward had ended his little brother's life and had never been held accountable.

Now a stranger had tried to find justice for Waylon, only to die as well.

He rubbed his forehead, not surprised when he heard the door opening and closing. Within seconds Grace was by his side.

"Sounds like this case just got personal," she surmised, open surprise in her tone.

"Yeah," he agreed grimly.

"You okay?"

He gave her a look. "No."

"If you'd said yes, I'd have called bullshit on you. So what now?"

Angelo closed his eyes, saw Waylon lying on the metal slab, his young body punctured by a bullet, his young life ended.

Anger, fresh and raw, choked out his ability to remain cool. He'd tried to find answers when Waylon had died but he'd come up empty, not that a nineteen-year-old kid had much to draw from, resource-wise.

Nothing—and everything—had changed.

"What's next?" Grace peered at him, waiting for his direction in light of the development. For all her tough appearance, Grace had a soft spot and apparently he'd found it. Maybe his face showed the shock he couldn't hide. He felt a hand on his shoulder. He turned and Grace offered a crooked smile. "Probably never saw that coming, huh?"

"Not by a mile," he admitted. *Shake it off, focus.* "Looks like we're going to need to spend a few more days with the tribe. You okay with that?"

Grace peered at him, her brown eyes knowing. "It's fine with me. The question is…is it fine with you?"

It'd have to be.

"We'll head back to Seattle for the time being. I need a few things before we come back."

"You got it."

As Angelo and Grace drove away, he couldn't escape the feeling at the back of his neck that he was on the precipice of something big, something that he could never walk away from again. He suppressed a shudder.

Maybe that's what had driven Hicks.

Angelo understood the drive, the passion for success and the subsequent frustration of failure.

Waylon's face flashed in his memory and his foot pressed harder on the gas pedal.

This time around failure wasn't an option.

There would be justice.

Chapter 9

Mya yawned and rubbed the fatigue from her eyes. Tonight was her turn on night shift and she was feeling the time pass slowly.

Iris walked up and handed her a steaming cup of coffee, which she accepted gratefully.

"How'd you know my caboose was dragging?" she asked, sipping at the coffee. She curled her hands around the cup, warming her fingers. "At least it's quiet."

Iris arched her brows. "Let's not tempt fate, shall we? I'd rather pass an uneventful evening than one filled with patients. Or, actually, I'd rather spend the evening snuggled in my bed next to that sexy brother of yours."

"Ack. Yes, he is my brother. Spare me the details of your love life, please. I'm tickled that you two finally found your way to one another but honestly, beyond that, I could live in blissful ignorance."

"Suit yourself," Iris said, grinning from above her

own cup. Her eyes lost their mirth as she broached a different subject. "So how are you doing? I heard about Porter."

Mya made a slight sound of annoyance. Damn, the reservation was small. She should have expected the news would travel fast. She managed a shrug. "We're moving in different directions…it's probably for the best."

"It seems rather sudden," Iris prompted, but Mya wasn't willing to take the bait. She tried harder. "I mean, it can't be complete coincidence that the minute Angelo shows up on the reservation, you suddenly have cold feet with Porter."

Mya tried to smother the flare of irritation; she knew Iris was only being honest, one of the traits she usually valued in her best friend. Tonight, not so much. She thought of lying, but in the end, Mya was pragmatic about things. Iris was bound to discover the truth so why delay the inevitable? She answered with a sigh, "What do you want me to say? If I say it had nothing to do with Angelo, chances are you won't believe me. If I say it had something to do with the man, then I'll get a lecture on how I should be moving on with a great guy like Porter. Either way, it's a lose-lose situation and one I have no interest in pursuing."

"So what I'm hearing you say is that you want me to back out of your business so you can figure things out on your own."

She smiled. "Yes, not in so many words but…yeah."

Iris returned a rueful smile. "I'll give it a whirl. I've never been good at minding my own business so I can't say I'll be successful, but…I'll try. Okay?" At Mya's nod, she added, more apologetically, "I worry. You're always taking such good care of everyone else but when it comes to yourself, you shortchange the one who matters the most. You were there for me unreservedly during my ordeal...I want to be there for you, too."

Unbidden tears sprang to Mya's eyes at Iris's mention of her "ordeal," which happened to be a brutal rape a year and a half ago, but she nodded and rushed to assure Iris because she didn't want her to think she was deliberately shutting her out. She just needed a little time to figure out where her head was. Or more specifically, her heart. "I love you, Iris, and I appreciate your offer. I know I always have you. And that means the world to me. I have a lot to sort out and, really, it's not fair to Porter to drag him through my messes in the hope that I might feel differently about the man when my head is finally on straight."

"I understand." Iris shrugged, admitting, "For what it's worth...I never really thought you were a good fit together."

"Oh, really? Then why the heavy matchmaking?"

Iris drained her cup and tossed it in the trash. "Because I hated the idea of you being hung up on Angelo and I knew if nothing else, Porter would make a great husband and father. Something we both know Angelo would not."

Iris left Mya with that final statement and it rang in Mya's ears. It was hard not to remember when she'd found out she was pregnant. Even harder to forget how she'd been devastated to discover the baby had died.

A lingering sadness threatened to pull her under but she shook it off as the sound of commotion in the front lobby drew her attention. Shouts and, it seemed, drunken hollering filled the quiet hum of the urgent care.

Looked like the lull was over.

* * *

Mya followed the sound of crashing carts and drunken blustering and found Darrick "Laughing Dog" Willets doing his level best to destroy her emergency room.

Two male nurses struggled to hold him down while Iris slipped in a wet spot that looked suspiciously like urine, swearing as her rear connected with the tiled floor. Mya suspected a darkened patch down Darrick's soiled pants would confirm her suspicion. She pulled on latex gloves and jumped into the fray.

"What's going on?" she asked one of the nurses as they grunted in their effort to restrain Darrick in a bed.

"He was wandering in the street and was hit by a car. He might have internal bleeding," Ivan said from between gritted teeth while his buddy Carl tied one arm down. "He's drunk as a skunk and a mean one at that."

Darrick wasn't usually a mean drunk. She'd known him his entire life. In fact, he'd been Waylon Tucker's best friend. He'd taken Waylon's death pretty hard and hadn't been the same since. Because of that, Mya had always treated him with kindness, though she couldn't say the rest of the tribe agreed with her. Most only saw a worthless drunk who more often than not wet himself when he passed out and generally caused a nuisance.

"Darrick," she said to him in a calm voice while he thrashed, spittle flying from his lips as he raved about things she couldn't discern. The man wasn't well on a good day: the extreme and persistent alcohol abuse had not only pickled his liver but his mind as well. "You need to be still so I can see if you're all right." Her voice, familiar enough to slide past the layers of alcohol haze, settled him, but he continued to strain against the restraints. She checked his pupils while Ivan checked his pulse and blood pressure. "Can you tell me what happened?"

"He's dead," he slurred. "Dead. I saw him fall into the water! Blood everywhere…washed away…gone forever. It's my fault!"

She steeled herself against the sadness that came when she thought of Waylon. "Waylon died a long time ago and it wasn't your fault, Darrick," she assured him in a soothing tone while Iris put an IV in. Darrick groaned when the needle entered his arm but at least he'd stopped yelling at the top of his lungs. Still, he mumbled under his breath—things she couldn't quite catch. "Darrick, I'm going to check you for injuries. You were struck by a car. Do you remember what happened?"

"I saw him. Need to talk to him," he managed on a groan. "It's my fault. All my fault. I need to tell him…"

"No broken bones but he's pretty scraped up. Go ahead and give him a light sedative so he can rest. The alcohol probably saved his life. He didn't tense up, just flopped onto the ground. I'd like to keep him for observation overnight."

"Poor Darrick," Iris murmured, rubbing her sore behind with a mild scowl. "Who knew he was going to end up like this?" She frowned slightly as she put the medicine into the IV. "I wonder what got him riled up? He hasn't gotten this sloppy drunk in a long time. The ghosts must be riding him pretty hard."

Mya nodded, trying to see the boy he used to be instead of the broken shell he'd become. His teeth were nearly rotted out of his head and his alcohol abuse had caused a terrible bleeding ulcer on top of the damage done to his liver. And, in spite of her warnings, he continued to drink himself to death, as if he welcomed the end and hoped to hasten it. Mya attributed his condition to Waylon's death. The two had been peas in a pod as kids.

"I don't know, maybe he happened to realize the anniversary of Waylon's death is only a few weeks away. But then, I doubt Darrick is fully aware of what day it is most times. Honestly, I'm amazed he hasn't died yet." Mya felt bad admitting it, but it was the truth. The man was defying the natural order of things. One might say he had a guardian spirit watching over him, but then you'd have to wonder why a guardian spirit would allow him to torture himself the way he did.

"Do you think Darrick happened to catch Angelo in town? Seeing Waylon's brother might be enough to trigger something."

"Maybe. I doubt it, though. Angelo wasn't on the rez long enough." She sighed, noting with quiet relief that the sedative had knocked Darrick out. "It's likely random. The poor man is being eaten alive by something that none of us can fathom. It's sad."

Iris agreed, adding wistfully, "Makes you wonder how different things might've been if Waylon hadn't died."

Mya swallowed a sudden lump in her throat. "Yeah." Waylon's death had been the cataclysm for so much in all their lives. Such sorrow... Mya shook off the grip of sadness and forced a smile. "Keep an eye on him. The alcohol level might work adversely with the sedative. I don't want him going under and not being able to come back out in the morning. Maybe tomorrow we can ask him some questions, if not, we should send him up to the mental health ward in Forks for evaluation."

Mya left Darrick in capable hands and headed for the

break room for some fresh coffee. She'd need a kick in the pants to get through the rest of the night.

Darrick's dreams were filled with disjointed images from the past blending with the present, until there was nothing but a nightmarish miasma of warped reality.

He heard Waylon's laughter, felt the sunshine on his bare shoulders, and knew the contentment of a teenage boy enjoying life. They'd caught a bucket full of crawfish and had grand plans to boil them up later that night at Waylon's place. This felt good...filled with happiness and joy.

Until Waylon's laughter was cut short, replaced by a sick gurgle and that horrifying splash. And Waylon was gone.

But then Waylon was back. Only now his friend was clearly dead, his normally robust skin pale and gray from the cold water of the Hoh and his eyes dull and lifeless, yet he stared at Darrick with accusation.

"Why'd you kill me?" Waylon asked, his watery voice slapping against Darrick like a sodden washcloth against a rock. "Why, brother?"

Darrick struggled against the hold the dream had on him, but the dream refused to let go. Suddenly Waylon reached for him, clamping down on his arm with a deathly cold grip, a dead man's grin on his face. Darrick struggled, screaming without sound.

"Nooo!"

His heart rate tripled dangerously, threatening cardiac arrest, but he couldn't pull free from his best friend's hold and Waylon continued to drag him closer to the water's edge.

"Join me, brother. It's only right."

"I'm sorry!" He pleaded with Waylon but the frigid

Hoh lapped at his sneakered feet, closing over the tops of his shoes. Cold water bit into his skin as he sank in the silt of the riverbank, losing traction as Waylon tugged him farther. "I loved you like a brother!" he screamed, fighting to keep his head above water.

Darrick lost Waylon's reply as the water closed over their heads.

And suddenly, darkness replaced everything.

Blessed darkness.

Chapter 10

Angelo returned to the reservation a few days later with enough provisions to hole up in his grandfather's home for as long as needed to solve the Hicks case. Grace was going to join him in a day or so, giving him time to take care of some personal business.

He hadn't thought it necessary, but Grace had disagreed, and once she got something into her head there was no hope of getting it out without a court order.

But as he'd finished unpacking, returning some semblance of livability to the old cabin, he realized perhaps Grace had been right.

There was one person on the reservation who'd been with him during that time when Waylon was killed—Mya—and he knew he'd have to talk to her.

He'd thought he could handle being around her in a professional capacity, but he'd been wrong.

Cool, efficient and utterly breathtaking, Mya had

grown into the woman he'd known she would, and while he accepted that he'd given up the right to notice a long time ago, he couldn't stop the pain that followed.

He remembered every moment they'd ever spent together in blinding detail, but he'd held on to the hope that perhaps with time he'd added embellishments that certainly couldn't hold up against the reality.

Surely her hair hadn't been like black cornsilk sliding through his fingers, her eyes like twin gems of onyx.

But seeing her again…he realized with sinking clarity his memory had been flawless when it came to Mya Jonson.

Angelo pushed his hand through his hair and moved to the room he'd shared with Waylon.

Papa had left it as it was when Waylon had died, and since he'd split soon after Papa had died, the room appeared suspended in time. Posters of their favorite things—motorbikes captured in midair, muscle cars and, of course, a few hot girls smiled from faded paper. He wandered without purpose. He wasn't usually such a masochist but he felt compelled to face what he'd run away from—if only to prove to himself that he could handle this case without losing his objectivity.

By all rights, he ought to hand the case over.

But he knew there was no way in hell that was going to happen.

Grace knew that, too. She was a good partner. She'd support him for as long as she could.

He went to the scarred desk, saw the bent tin cup they'd kept odds and ends in—pencils, a few paper clips and pennies, and opened the drawers. The smell of aged wood and simpler times tickled his nose. Finding it empty, he closed the drawers and leaned against the desk.

Something black scurried across the hardwood planks of the floor. He sighed. It would take more than a few sweeps of the broom to get this place truly livable. Thank God he wasn't staying that long.

Mya had just woken from her nap after the night shift when she heard a car come up her drive. She grabbed a sweatshirt and pulled it over her thin chemise and then jerked on some old sweatpants.

She glanced out her window and when she didn't recognize the car she frowned, ignoring the shiver of apprehension that followed. She didn't get many visitors aside from Sundance and Iris and she knew neither would show up after she'd worked the night shift and was likely sleeping. So that meant whoever was coming up the drive didn't necessarily know her personally. Mya glanced down at the baseball bat she kept by the front door, reassured by its presence. After the serial rapist had attacked Iris in her home, Mya couldn't help the twinge of anxiety at unannounced visitors and, although she couldn't see herself getting a gun, she did have the presence of mind to know that some kind of self-defense was smart.

It wasn't long before a short rap on the front door caused her to jump. With a gulp of air, she opened the door, but not the chain lock. She wasn't prepared to see Angelo standing there.

"Can I talk to you?" he asked, looking intensely uncomfortable. "It's important."

The irrational side of her urged her to shut the door and tell him she'd long since stopped being his confidante, but she couldn't bring herself to actually do that. For one, it would be rude; second, she was curious about what would prompt Angelo to seek her out. Still, she wasn't keen on spending alone time with the man, either, if even to satisfy that curiosity. "I'm pretty tired," she said, grudgingly sliding open the chain. "Make it quick, please."

"No time for niceties, I see," he said with a hard smile that only flirted with the impression of being courteous. She closed the door behind him and walked briskly to the living room, hating that he was behind her and she couldn't help but wonder if he was looking at her butt. Worse, perhaps, was the idea that he *wasn't* looking at her butt.

Annoyed with herself, she replied coolly, "I can't imagine what we have to talk about, Angelo. I think we said all that needed to be said the day you left." *Left me weeping, alone and abandoned.* A hot rush of remembered humiliation accosted her cheeks and she lifted her chin, daring him to make a comment. She wasn't that sad, broken-hearted girl any longer. She'd long since stopped wetting her pillow with tears for Angelo. And if that odd yearning in her chest thrummed with melancholy sadness it wasn't because she still loved him— Great Spirit help her if she were that stupid—it was just an ache born of sacrifice and responsibility. Nothing more. "So let's get this over with," she snapped.

His expression was one of sharp disagreement but he gave away nothing. Whatever was going on behind those eyes, he didn't betray it. She wore hostility like body armor but a faint sad smile threatened as she thought how wide the gap had stretched between them. There was a time when she'd known by the flick of his gaze the bend of his thoughts. She shifted in her baggy sweatpants, overly aware of how grubby and shabby she appeared. *So what? Why should I care what he thinks of the way I'm dressed?* She flattened her lips in

irritation—whether at herself or him she wasn't sure—
and waited for him to get on with whatever mission had
brought him there.

Angelo drew a deep breath as if not sure how to
begin. In the end, he went with the direct approach,
which was much more like him anyway. He'd never
been one to dance around an issue. "It's like this…the
case I've been assigned—"

"The dead agent," she interjected briskly.

He nodded, continuing, "Seems he was doing some
rogue investigating into a cold case—" he met her gaze
squarely "—specifically, into Waylon's case."

She inhaled sharply even as she stared. Waylon?
"Why would a stranger care about the tribe's personal
tragedy?" Some of her hostility lessened as she considered how this newfound information must've kicked
Angelo in a raw spot. She didn't want to but she couldn't
help but feel something for Angelo for the situation he
was in. "I don't understand. Waylon's case wasn't within
FBI jurisdiction."

"Seems he thought if he managed to crack the case
he might get some kudos from the higher-ups who kept
passing him over for promotion," he answered with a
bitter twist of his mouth. Angelo clearly hated that
Hicks had been trying to use his brother's case for his
own gain.

"How awful," she said, a low throbbing pain beginning to pulse in her forehead as she remembered
Waylon. She could still see his handsome face, hear
his mischievous laugh whenever he pulled a prank or
told a joke, and feel the pride he wore for his tribe.
"Oh, damn." She wanted to remain apart from any pain
Angelo might be feeling, but she couldn't help wanting
to reach out to him for what he must be suffering. She

leaned forward to rest her forearms on her knees. "So I imagine you'll be removed from the case?"

"Technically, I should be, but my director is giving me some latitude."

"That's kind. I didn't realize the FBI had a soft side."

"They don't. If word gets out that I'm heading this case, I'll get pulled, but for the time being, while it remains low-profile, I'll do what I can. That's why I need your help."

She stared. "What?"

"You and I both know that I'm persona non grata around the reservation. You, on the other hand, are the tribe's most trusted member. If I start asking questions, doors will slam in my face. If you're with me, maybe they'll listen and help."

She stiffened as his request sank in. And just as quickly as she understood, her refusal followed. "I'm not a lucky rabbit's foot. You can't just drag me around in the hopes of easing the tribe's opinion of you. You made your bed long ago, Angelo. Besides, you overestimate my ability to sway people in your direction. There's not much I can do for you."

"Mya, I would never ask for myself. I'm asking for Waylon."

Damn sneaky bastard. How could he so easily play that card? Had he no shame? He knew she couldn't refuse when he put it like that. She'd loved Waylon as deeply as she loved her own brother. She'd taken it for granted that someday she and Angelo would marry and then Waylon would become her brother anyway. When he'd died, she'd felt the blow to her heart, too. Tears glittered in her eyes but she narrowed her gaze at Angelo, communicating what she thought of his tactics. "That was uncalled for. I would ask that you not stoop to such emotional manipulation again when asking for a favor. I don't respond well to such maneuvers."

He didn't even have the grace to flush. Instead he boldly held her gaze as if her cold reply hadn't touched him at all. And, in fact, it hadn't. "Mya, let's cut the crap. You don't like me, I hear you loud and clear on that score, but I'm not going anywhere until I get some answers. If you want me out of here, help me find what I need, and I'll be gone." Then he added with a dark mumble, "It's not like this place is brimming with great memories for me."

She blinked back sudden tears. Wasn't *she* part of those memories? They'd been dating nearly their entire childhood up until the point when he'd split, leaving her and everyone else behind like a bad habit. Mya willed the tears away—she damn well wasn't going to allow him to see her cry—and rose stiffly, her very frame vibrating with pent-up anger, grief and maybe remorse. "Angelo...did you ever take the time to consider that maybe if you hadn't abandoned everyone, you might have those very doors you want to access open to you just as they are to me? The tribe's cold shoulder is a consequence of your actions. I cannot help you with that. You're on your own. Now, if you please, I want you to leave."

Angelo's face darkened, betraying the rise in his blood pressure, but he offered a curt nod to her request. She almost wished he'd rail at her, demand that she help him, something other than the icy contained composure. Perhaps if she caught a glimpse of something that pulsed with life—pain, guilt, agony—she'd rest knowing that he wasn't as stoic as he seemed, that she wasn't the only one suspended in limbo, unable to move forward.

But how selfish was she for refusing to help for purely personal reasons? *Great Spirit, help me.* Could she stand to work with Angelo in the short term in the hopes of finally finding Waylon's killer?

She caught her bottom lip in her teeth, indecision grabbing her as he walked to the door. He'd get nowhere with the tribe. He'd leave with nothing. They'd clam up as surely as they would with a stranger, no matter that it was the hereditary chief asking the questions.

It seemed the choice was simple.

"Wait," she said, gritting her teeth against the urge to spit the words at him. He turned, faint surprise marring his handsome face. "I'll help. Waylon deserves justice. I'm doing it for him. Not you."

Angelo regarded her for a long moment and then nodded. A sardonic grin graced his sensual mouth. "I wouldn't dare dream otherwise." He walked out the door toward his vehicle, saying over his shoulder, as if throwing her a bone when, in fact, he ought to be thanking her for her kindness. "I'll be in touch." And then he was gone.

Mya glowered at the retreating vehicle for longer than necessary, and then, when she couldn't see the car any longer, she slammed the front door.

You're doing this for Waylon, she reminded herself darkly.

Angelo could go to hell.

Chapter 11

Words he should've offered a long time ago—explanation, apology, all of those things—died behind his teeth, unsaid.

Angelo drove away from Mya's little house, mired in feelings he routinely pushed away, and tried to regain focus. She said she'd help. That was something. He wasn't naive and he'd spoken the truth. Memories were long around here and doors would not open for him. No matter his cause.

A memory sprang to life of him ridiculing the old ways, embarrassing Papa with his open disdain for a heritage he felt no kinship with and causing a painful rift between himself and Waylon.

He'd often wondered how he and his brother could share DNA when they were so different.

"White Arrow, you are the next chief. This is a great honor that you bear for your tribe," Papa had said to him the night he'd deliberately ignored Papa's request to join him at Council—again. "We are a dying tribe. It is our responsibility to remember the old ways, to breathe life into the bones of our ancestors through the stories we tell our children. You are strong and smart. This is your duty, boy," Papa had said ardently, his eyes sad but frustrated as well.

"No one asked me if I wanted this *honor*," Angelo had sneered, hating that everyone assumed he'd take on the role—which had no real meaning anyway aside from the ceremonial—when he had his own dreams and aspirations that didn't start and stop on tribal land. "Pick someone else. I'm not interested. It's not my deal. Give it to Waylon. He cares about that stupid legend shit anyway. I don't."

And then he'd stormed from the house, intent on living his life his own way without anyone pressuring him to do anything more than what he wanted.

Of course, he'd been full of teenage bluster and angst. And his mouth had spewed words honed to a fine edge.

A sigh escaped from deep within his chest. He wished he hadn't been so harsh with Papa. His grandfather had been a good man. It wasn't his fault he'd been saddled with two grandkids to raise because his own son had turned out to be a worthless drunk.

And then Waylon—his one chance at putting things right—had died, and Angelo had been a poor consolation.

At least that's how it felt, even after all these years.

Mya had been better off without him. Of that, at least, he was confident.

He'd find justice for Waylon and Hicks and then he'd finally walk away from the tribe for good.

It was best for everyone.

* * *

Mya strode purposefully to her office, her mind jumping from one scenario to another with dizzying speed as she considered all the different possibilities, including working with Angelo in the short term as well as the logistics of calling in her replacement for a few days. She had plenty of personal time, a sad consequence of not having a life, and helping the FBI shouldn't interfere with work at all.

However, rearranging her feelings during that short time period was a much more daunting aspect.

"Talk to me," Iris demanded as she entered Mya's office while she was finishing her leave paperwork. Iris plopped into the chair by the desk and pinned Mya with a steady and mildly unnerving gaze. "Out with it. What the hell is going on?"

There was no reason to lie. Mya had nothing to hide. "I'm helping Angelo with his case." She made short work of explaining the circumstances, continuing as she slipped the paperwork in the fax and hit Send. "Seems the agent who was killed was investigating Waylon's case. You and I both know that without my help Angelo wouldn't get very far with the tribe, so, in the interest of expediency, I'm going to help out."

"I don't like it," Iris said flatly, leaving no mystery as to where her feelings landed on that score. "You need to avoid him all together and let him figure things out on his own. This is a bad idea."

"I'm a grown woman, Iris," Mya chided her friend lightly, amused—to a point—that Iris was so protective. "He's not the big bad wolf. He's just a man and this is more about Waylon than it is Angelo. I loved the boy, too."

The reminder softened the rigid set of Iris's shoulders.

Everyone had liked Waylon. "I know you loved Waylon—we all loved Waylon. He was a great kid and if he'd been able to grow up, he would've been one hell of an adult, but just because we all had a soft spot for Waylon doesn't mean that Angelo can use those feelings to get what he needs for his job."

"It's not like that," Mya said, frowning. "Bottom line, a man died and his death is directly related to Waylon's unsolved case. Which means that a killer is on the loose on the reservation. Perhaps with my help, Angelo can catch this person and finally put Waylon to rest. I'm willing to do that for a boy I loved dearly."

Iris's mouth twitched darkly. "Which boy? Angelo or Waylon?"

Mya glowered. "Waylon."

"Are you sure? Because this seems like something a woman might do if she were, oh, still totally hung up on a guy. In fact, I might've seen this plot in a movie once," she quipped with a snort. "Come on, Mya. This smacks of a bad idea. Even you've got to admit that if this were anyone else and the shoe were on the other foot, you'd say the same thing. I mean, *you're* the logical one, for crying out loud."

"He needs my help," Mya maintained stubbornly, but Iris's stab at logic did make a lot of sense. Well, it was too late to back out now. The paperwork had been submitted and she never did anything that made her appear wishy-washy. So, better or worse, she was going to see this through to the end and stick to her agreement to help. "Besides, what do you think is going to happen in the space of a few days? He's going to fall to his knees, profess his undying love for me and that declaration is going to cause me to forget the last fifteen years? Well, let me ease your fears, however irrational.

I'm not interested in Angelo Tucker. I am interested in finding who is the snake amongst us before he kills someone else. I promise that is my only motivation."

"I'd feel a whole lot more secure in your promise if you were happily married with kids." Mya stiffened involuntarily and Iris reacted with swift apology. "That was insensitive of me. I'm so sorry. Forget that part. What I mean to say is—"

Mya reached out and covered Iris's hand with her own, smiling briefly. "I know what you were trying to say. Let it be. It's fine. Stop worrying. I need you focused so you can help my replacement for a few days. You're my right hand around here."

"Who are you requesting?" Iris asked, resigned to Mya's decision and moving on to details pertinent to the moment. "Please not Dr. Billingham," she said with distaste. "He has sweaty palms and I can only sanitize my hands so many times in one hour before people start to ask if I'm OCD."

Mya cracked a grin. "Lucky you, he wasn't available. Looks like Dr. Solvang is going to step in. You like him, right?"

"He'll do. For a few days," Iris grumbled with bad humor, adding with a narrowed gaze. "Please try to remember that Angelo broke your heart and never looked back. Forget about what happened with the tribe. What he did to you is what matters. Nothing he could say or do will change that. Okay?"

Mya nodded, a lump rising in her throat. "That's not something I could ever forget," she promised quietly.

She'd suffered more than a broken heart—it'd felt as if her soul had cracked in two.

And that was pretty damn hard to get over.

* * *

Angelo waited in his car, off the road at the put-in spot for kayakers and other river recreationers who enjoyed the scenic ride of the spring runoff on the Hoh River. She'd suggested meeting at the rinky-dink diner—a greasy spoon of the lowest order guaranteed to upset your gut on a good day—but he'd wanted a little privacy for their first meeting. He wasn't sure of her attitude and wanted to test things out first. It was best to come at an unknown with some kind of advantage, and he didn't relish an audience just in case things went sour.

His pulse jumped when her car rolled up next to his. He exited his vehicle as she did the same. They were both wrapped in warm clothing to combat the misty cold, but the brisk air immediately put roses in her cheeks and plumed in a frosty curl as she offered a curt greeting. She shoved gloved hands into her thick wool coat, shaking her head at his choice. "A diner would've been warmer," she said. "We might catch our death out here."

He didn't want to notice how her full hips tapered to slim legs clad in dark-blue denim, or how those same jeans clung to the delectable roundness of her rear. The cold air didn't seem to cool his blood enough to stop the thoughts from traveling to unwelcome places. They'd lost their virginity together. What an embarrassing, fumbling idiot he'd been that first time. He'd been amazed—and grateful—that she'd been willing to try it a second time. And a third. Eventually, they'd found their rhythm and things had improved. He smothered the smile that threatened, knowing with certainty that she wouldn't appreciate the topic of his amusement. It's not like he could admit that he still harbored those kinds of thoughts about her. Hell, he could hardly admit it to himself. It must be the place. Nostalgia was probably only natural.

"Angelo? Did you hear me?" she asked, bringing him back to the present to find her peering at him with a frown. "Are you feeling all right? You look flushed."

"I'm not one of your patients. No need to fuss over me, Doctor," he said with a dismissive shake of his head. He was more annoyed at himself for drifting. "I know it's cold and you're right, the diner or someplace indoors probably would've been best, but I didn't want an audience."

"An audience for what?" she asked, crossing her arms and staring him down.

He gestured. "This. You're still a little touchy about the past and I didn't know how well this meeting was going to go."

She huffed a breath of pure annoyance. "Get over yourself, Angelo. Let's get on with it so we don't freeze. I have no interest in being a patient in my own clinic because I've suffered hypothermia."

"It's not that cold," he groused, even as he burrowed deeper into his coat. He leaned against the grill of his car, briefly taken in by the lush beauty of his homeland. He'd never cared before, never noticed, but there was a savage splendor to the Olympic National Forest that was simply unlike any other place. Waylon would've said it was because they had roots that went down deep into the soil, but Angelo wasn't willing to go that far. He just finally appreciated the natural beauty. He glanced Mya's way, noting how she kept to her car instead of joining him at his. He pushed at the pang of sadness that followed. Damn. Forget the beauty, this place was like a poison, leaking into his bloodstream.

Why else would he be plagued by this constant feeling that he'd lost out on something truly amazing when he'd walked away?

"You never married. Makes me wonder why," he said, looking away, hating that he'd even said the words, but they'd fell from his lips as if springing to be free. As selfish as it was, a small part of him had the audacity to hope that he was the reason she hadn't taken that step yet. Of course, he wasn't brave enough to admit that so he simply offered her a mocking shrug. "I mean, it's none of my business. I was just curious."

Her silence tugged at him, forcing him to meet her gaze. "Are we here to talk about Waylon or why you ran away from everyone you'd ever cared about?" Her stare was sharp enough to pierce skin and he felt schooled. "We can have either conversation but I came to talk about Waylon."

He angled toward her, calling her bluff, though he wasn't sure why. It was pure lunacy and an exercise in pain for the two of them, but he couldn't back down from that steady stare. "And what if I wanted to talk about us? Would you be willing to talk about that?"

Her mouth firmed and he was almost sure she was going to tell him to go to hell, but she didn't. "Angelo, let's just stick to Waylon. It's safer."

"You always were about being safe," he murmured, earning a swift and caustic reply in return.

"And you were always about yourself. Seems not much has changed."

Ah, damn. She wasn't pulling any punches. Not that he expected her to. Mya wore professional civility well but underneath that lab coat a warrior spirit lurked. He'd do well to remember that before he ended up on the wrong end of her weapon of choice. "Seems I was

wise in not going somewhere public for this meeting."
He shrugged off the guilt that was skewering him along
with her gaze and said, "All right, enough. We both have
regrets. We'll leave it at that. Are you ready to do this?"

The corners of her mouth twitched with a smile but
her eyes remained cold and distant as she answered, "Of
course. I came to find answers. You're the one wasting
time."

"Touché." He pushed off the grille. "Let's go then.
I figured we'd hit the bait and tackle shop first. Byron
Hicks came ostensibly to fish and you can't fish with-
out supplies."

"The old bait shop is gone," she said. "It was washed
away a few years ago by the flooding. Now Bunny sells
bait through his home."

Angelo digested the information. "The flooding got
that bad?"

"Yes. There are many who have lost their homes.
Before long any home near the river's edge will be gone.
We're trying to acquire more land in the tribe's name
so we can relocate the homes but it's been slow."

Angelo thought of the people he remembered who
lived closest to the river. "Who all has lost their homes?"
he asked, feeling the weight of his people's misfortune
on his shoulders no matter how many years ago he'd
shrugged off the responsibility. "Richards? Cannuck?
Erwin?"

His recollection earned him a shrewd look even
as she nodded. "Yes. Some have moved in with other
family members, others, such as the Erwins, simply
moved away. It was very sad, but what choice did they
have?"

None. It was probably wise for everyone to leave, but
he knew some would rather die on their native soil than

live elsewhere. Like Mya. "What's the Council doing to get someone in the right places to listen?"

"They're doing all they can," she said, her brusque reply enough to remind him that these were not his worries and he could do nothing to help.

"Well, I hope it works out," he said, hating how flip he sounded, but it wouldn't do to start fighting battles he had no stake in. Besides, he loathed hypocrites and he wouldn't become one just to ease the suffocating pressure on his chest. As soon as he got away from this place, it would ease. "So where does Bunny live now?"

"Up the bend. We can walk there." She didn't wait, simply started walking.

He had no choice but to follow or get left behind.

Chapter 12

Mya kept a brisk pace, angry with herself for sharing the personal troubles of the tribe with a man who had shunned his own heritage routinely as a kid and clearly hadn't changed much in the years of adulthood that followed.

But she'd been incensed by the implication that they were all sitting around wringing their hands, hoping and praying someone was going to swoop in and save them. Who was he to judge when he'd walked away without a second glance so many years ago?

If he'd stayed, he would have taken his rightful place at the head of the Council and been among the decision-makers of the tribe instead of the ragtag group that reluctantly took to the helm. They needed guidance, a strong hand to unite them. But they had to work with what they had, and Mya tried to be grateful for the volunteers who had stepped up. How could she explain to someone who cared for nothing that pride in one's heritage was about more than checking a box on a government form? It was about preserving the legacy that flowed through their veins, making the tribe strong again when so many generations had fallen to the evils of alcohol and drugs. It was about guiding their young folk and instilling that same sense of pride that had beat so strongly inside the heart of Waylon Tucker.

All of these things were foreign to Angelo and it was her deep disappointment that choked her ability to remain detached and professional.

Angelo caught up easily, his breathing hardly taxed, and they walked side by side in silence for a long moment. As teenagers they'd spent plenty of time on the river. It was difficult to ignore the press of memories as they traversed the soft, spongy ground, verdant with mossy undergrowth and smelling of dark, rich soil. The summer they'd discovered each others' bodies the river had been their favorite spot for privacy. Her breath hitched as one particular memory persisted and she struggled to hide her distressing reaction.

She could almost feel the coarse scratch of the woven blanket cushioned by the soft grass under her bottom, could hear the rush of the river. His hands, reverent and gentle but shaking with a boy's impatience, touched her breast as his mouth descended on hers. Her thoughts had blurred and melted as her skin came alive under his touch. Was there anything more glorious, more amazing than the discovery of something magical with someone for whom your heart beats? She knew the answer, but as it gave her joy then, it only caused heartache now.

"We're almost there," she managed to say, surprised that her voice sounded steady when inside she was a quaking mess. Iris had been right. Damn the woman for knowing her so well. She stopped and squared off with Angelo, briefing him. "Bunny is basically harmless, but he's an alcoholic and sometimes he has a temper that flares when he's been on a bender."

"I remember Bunny," Angelo said, his tone patient, even slightly patronizing, and she bristled.

"Good, then you won't be surprised if he tries to take a swing at you."

"Why would he do that? I've been gone for years."

"Precisely." She shrugged. "It's as good a reason as any. Besides, if you recall, Bunny had a soft spot for your grandfather. He doesn't think too highly of you for abandoning the tribe."

"Wonderful."

At that she smiled. "Hopefully, the FBI taught you something about self-defense?"

His mouth turned down but he jerked his head as if to say, *move on,* which she did.

A rickety cabin came into view and a few dogs bayed and howled, announcing their presence. Angelo, ever alert, kept his eye on the dogs in case they weren't friendly but he needn't have worried. Mya had made plenty of house calls to Bunny's house over the years, and the dogs would recognize her scent. Sure enough, Redbone and Delilah, Bunny's hounds, ambled over to her and licked her fingers as she went to pet them. "Sorry, no treats today," she told them as she patted their heads, flashing a smile at Angelo. "Don't worry, their bark is far worse than their bite."

"I wasn't worried," he said stiffly, yet he didn't attempt to pet either dog as they walked to the front door.

Before they could knock, Bunny's wife, Hettie, opened the door and scowled when she saw them.

"What do you want? Nobody called you."

"Hello, Hettie," Mya said in a conversational tone, smiling in spite of the woman's unwelcoming expression. "We're here to talk to Bunny. Is he home?"

"He ain't got no job. Where else he gonna be?" Hettie said sullenly before hollering for her husband. "Stay outside. I didn't prepare for no visitors."

Hettie wasn't much of a house cleaner and certainly not much of a wife, but she and Bunny had been brawling together since before Mya was born; she figured the two were cut from the same cloth and simply accepted things as they were.

Bunny emerged from the house, a waft of cigarette smoke and stale beer following him, and peered at Mya first. He stretched, popping his back with a grunt. "Whatcha doing here, Doc?" he asked, in a tone slightly more friendly than that of his wife's. Then his gaze settled on Angelo and as soon as recognition set in his mouth pinched and his eyes became hostile. "You lost, boy?"

Mya stepped forward, not interested in fueling the fire when it would take little to fan it into an inferno with Bunny. "We need your help," Mya said, grabbing Bunny's attention. Bunny liked to feel needed, important. It wasn't often that he felt either. "It's about Waylon."

Bunny blinked as if hearing the name caused a pain somewhere deep under the skin and his shoulders sagged. "What about Waylon? He's long dead. More's the pity." Angelo's face darkened but he held his tongue. Mya felt a tiny bit of sympathy for Angelo. It had to be hard to be the one person nobody felt any kinship with. Bunny ignored Angelo and looked to Mya. "So what's going on? Has it got something to do with him?" He gestured to Angelo and spared him a short look.

"Yes. Angelo is here investigating the death of another man, special agent Byron Hicks. You might've sold bait to him. He'd come to the Hoh on vacation to fish."

Bunny rubbed the salt-and-pepper stubble on his brown weathered chin and searched his memory. There weren't many tourists to this stretch of land, so it was unlikely Bunny didn't remember, but he was taking his time for his own reasons. Mya could only wait and see. "What's some tourist got to do with Waylon?"

"Special Agent Hicks was doing more than fish the Hoh. He was investigating Waylon's cold case. We think that's what got him killed."

"I didn't kill no agent if that's where you're headed," he shot back, suddenly on the defensive. "And I loved Waylon like a son. He was a good boy."

Mya soothed him with a soft touch, murmuring, "No one is accusing you of anything. We need your help, remember?"

Bunny settled but he remained twitchy. He was probably jonesing for a drink right about now but they needed him sober. "Yeah, I remember the guy. Sold him some flashtrap spinners and some salmon-egg bait cure. He paid cash for it 'cuz I told him I didn't take no fancy credit cards or checks from strangers."

"Did he say anything at all about investigating the old case?" Angelo asked.

"No. Not that I remember, but I was a few beers into the day by that point. Maybe Hettie would remember. She talked him up some when I went back to get the egg bait cure."

"Would you mind asking her to speak with us?" Mya asked with an encouraging smile, switching subjects for the moment to keep him talking. "Bunny, have you been to the clinic for your annual blood work?"

"Been trying. No money for the check-up," he groused, clearly embarrassed by his financial situation. This was common among the older generation, while the younger generation seemed to flaunt their lack of ability to pay for services. Bunny lifted his arm and jerked up his sleeve, exposing a nasty sore on his forearm. "Got this a few months ago and the damn thing won't heal for nothing. Hurts like a son of a bitch, too."

She drew closer, not liking the red, angry wound that seeped and oozed around the edges of the scab. "What happened?"

"I lost my footing on a rock and fell, scraped it pretty good."

"Damn near drowned is what you did." Hettie's strident tone cut through the cold air as she appeared in the doorway. "I had to haul him out of the river like a fish caught on a line. Should've left you there to rot, you drunk," she said with a sniff.

Case forgotten for the moment, Mya peered at the wound. "Bunny, you need to let me take a biopsy of that. It doesn't look good. A regular cut should've healed by now. I want to see you first thing tomorrow morning at the clinic."

For all her bluster, faint worry lines bracketed Hettie's eyes as she came up behind Bunny, her arms crossed at her ample chest. "I told him it didn't look good. And while you're there, you better tell her about how sick you've been feeling."

"Shut up, will you?" he said sharply, causing his wife to scowl. "They ain't here to listen to me whine. I told you I felt fine."

Hettie ignored him and tattled on him anyway. "He's

been throwing up a lot. It's real bad in the spring. Seems to throw up when he spends too much time near the water."

"That's just plain stupid. I told you then and I'm telling you now, ain't no one gotten sick just by being near the river!" Bunny bellowed. "I've been splashing around in the Hoh since I was smaller than a deer tick, now answer the doc's questions so they can get on out of here. They look ready to freeze to death."

Angelo's gaze sharpened. "How long have you been getting sick after spending time in the water?"

Bunny waved him off. "It's nothing. An old woman's superstition."

"Humor us," Mya said softly.

Uncomfortable but unable to deny Mya's request, he said with a shrug, "Off and on for a few years now. Been real bad lately, probably in the last three years. Been so bad this last year I haven't hardly done any fishing."

Angelo and Mya exchanged looks. "First thing tomorrow, Bunny, I need to run some labs, see what's happening in your system."

He looked as nervous as Hettie but still he tried to slough it off. "Pah. It ain't nothing but my old bones acting up."

"It's more than that and you know it," Hettie hissed, risking a jittery look Mya's way that Angelo caught.

"What do you think it is?" he asked Hettie.

Put on the spot she balked and buttoned up. "I ain't saying nothing," she said, backing into the house. "I know what's good for me."

"Hettie…" Mya called out but the door had already slammed.

Bewildered, Mya looked to Bunny but he'd started to make his excuses, too. "I'll come in tomorrow. I promise. I don't know what to tell you about that agent. I sold him some fishing stuff and sent him on his way. That's it. That's all I know."

"But you said Hettie—"

Bunny cut Angelo off with a hard glare. "I didn't say nothing about nothing. Now get off my property before I call the rez cop."

Mya hated when people called her brother a rez cop. It was insulting and rude, but Bunny was already agitated by something and it wasn't likely to get better if she reminded him that Sundance was good to him and deserved better treatment. A fight for another day, she supposed with a weary sigh. She gestured to Angelo as she waved to Bunny. "I'll see you tomorrow," she said by way of encouraging him to actually show up, which she highly doubted he would. She could only hope Bunny made it to the clinic. She hadn't been kidding when she'd said she was worried about that wound. It didn't look normal at all. In fact, it didn't look like a wound caused by a scrape, either. Hard to know for sure without taking some tests, which would be impossible without Bunny's cooperation.

Angelo and Mya started walking back to their cars.

"What do you think they're hiding?" Angelo asked.

She shrugged. "No telling. They're old and superstitious and drunk half the time. It's really hard to put much store in what they have to say, but I am concerned about that sore."

Angelo disagreed on her first point. "Hettie was scared and Bunny had an idea why. We'll need to find a way to question them separately. I could haul them in but something tells me that'll cause them to clam up pretty quick."

"You got that right. It needs to be finessed if you

want Bunny and Hettie's cooperation. They've been on the river a long time. They're used to just being around each other."

"Well, they know something and I need to know what it is," Angelo said darkly. "I know when someone's spooked and those two were nearly shaking in their moccasins. What would cause them to be so afraid?"

Mya bit her bottom lip. "Good question," she murmured. Angelo made a good point and her instincts agreed with his suspicions. The older duo was hiding something, and she suspected it was connected to that sore on Bunny's arm. "We'll come back tomorrow. I have a feeling Bunny's not going to find himself a way to the clinic, so the clinic will just have to come to him. I'll bring Iris and Sundance for backup and while I'm tending to Bunny, you can question Hettie."

The corners of Angelo's mouth tilted in a slow, appreciative smile that sent a zing straight down to her toes. "I like your style. That sounds like an excellent plan," he said. "Now let's just hope they don't find it in them to skip the reservation before then."

Mya scoffed at that idea, but she'd never seen Hettie and Bunny so openly agitated. She rubbed at her arms. "Let's get out of this cold. Bunny was right—I'm about to freeze to death."

Chapter 13

Angelo's head was filled with questions, but there was more than what should've been swirling around his thoughts. In short, it was Mya.

He'd always known Mya had a strength about her, but seeing her in action with Bunny had tipped his appreciation just a bit further in the wrong direction. He didn't need to feel more for Mya—he already felt too much.

"When's your partner coming back?" Mya asked, breaking into his private musings. They'd reached their cars and he was reluctant to leave, but he walked with deliberate purpose to his car as Mya went to hers.

"Tomorrow afternoon. She's getting caught up on some details on another case for the time being," he answered, fidgeting with his keys. A night of solitude stared back at him and he didn't like it one bit. It was being back in this place, he thought with a wash of irritation, not Mya that made him antsy and nostalgic. "Thanks for your help," he offered and Mya graced him with a smile. He swallowed, wishing for selfish reasons that Mya hadn't aged well. Maybe that would've made things easier for him. Likely not. It was impossible for Mya to look anything but breathtaking. It was her spirit, it shone through her skin and gave her a glow unlike anyone else. And once she'd reserved that special spark for him. Not anymore. He'd royally stomped into the ground something beautiful and there was no repairing what he'd destroyed. He knew that and had long ago come to terms with it—so why was he struggling with this desperate longing?

"Well, I should get going…" Mya opened her car door to climb inside and he found himself compelled to persuade her to come with him back to his place. Hunger—hot and reckless and certainly dangerous—ate away at his good sense and pushed him to want what he didn't deserve. Mya peered at him with a frown. "Is something wrong?" she asked.

Yes. *Everything.* What was wrong with him? What could he say? Sharp regret had him by the short hairs? Somehow he didn't think such a declaration would go over very well. How about *I miss you more than I ever imagined I would and being here now is a special kind of torture.* Torture he had certainly earned for walking away like an idiot. "I just wondered if you'd like to come back to my place and go over some notes with me," he lied—well, not a complete lie, but certainly not the entire truth. He forced a shrug when she simply stared in response. "I mean, nothing personal, of course. I just figured two heads were better than one when recalling the past, and since you were with me when Waylon was found, I thought you might be able to remember details I wouldn't. But if you don't feel comfortable…"

Her frozen expression lost some of its rigidity, but he wasn't surprised when she stiffly declined.

"I don't think that's wise," she said, ducking to get into the car.

"Why not?" he dared, cursing himself for not adhering to good sense when clearly he was out of his mind at the moment. Her refusal smacked his pride but it also plucked at the wild, unpredictable nature of the feelings he kept under lock and key. How was it that she could be so unmoved by their past? Was he the only one who suffered regrets? They should've hashed this out a long time ago. Perhaps then they wouldn't have to deal with the distraction of unfinished business. "Clearly, we're both adults and working together for a common goal. I can handle it, if you can."

It was a mild taunt, pushing at the well-hidden button of competition that she'd harbored since they were kids. He ought to feel shame for manipulating her this way, but instead he felt the tingle of victory as she wavered, clearly struggling with good sense and the need to win. Her mouth firmed and she lifted her chin. "I'll be there in an hour—on one condition. No talk of the past as it pertained to you and me. Got it?"

He smothered a smile, knowing it would likely cause her to change her mind, and nodded gravely. "Of course. Strictly business. Like I said, it shouldn't be a problem. Not for me anyway."

"And it won't be for me," she said icily. Before he could retort, she slammed her door and drove away.

Angelo let out a pent-up breath, laughing softly even as his hands shook, betraying just how much he'd been holding back, pretending not to care when, in fact, a part of him wanted to grab her and kiss her to make up for time lost. That would likely go over *very* badly.

He climbed into his own car. Tonight ought to be interesting, at the very least.

Mya's heart raced, almost tripping over itself in a rapid staccato, nearly beating out a message that translated to: Bad idea! Bad idea!

And she heard it loud and clear but she wasn't going to be that sad, sorry woman who couldn't bear to be around the man who broke her heart—a million years ago—and who fell into a sobbing heap because he happens to show up all of a sudden. If he could be aloof and distant, she could be equally so.

She blasted into the urgent care facility to check in with Dr. Solvang, and, finding everything in order and moving smoothly, she detoured to her office to write a few notes for the nurses when she found Iris coming from the staff lounge. She mentally winced when Iris came at her with a big grin. "Drinks at your place, right? Sundance is working late—" Iris saw Mya's chagrin and her smile fell. "You're canceling on me?"

"I'm so sorry, something came up," Mya said, dancing around the true reason until she realized she had nothing to hide. "Angelo and I are going to go over notes from the case."

Iris's displeasure rippled across her beautiful face; even in anger the woman was jaw-droppingly gorgeous. Mya resisted the urge to take a pass with the lipgloss across her own lips when she realized that would only look highly suspect in her best friend's eyes. "For a smart woman, you're being very dumb," Iris stated flatly.

Mya made a face. "Thank you. But I'm fine. I know what I'm doing."

"Yeah, you're going to be *doing* Angelo in about three hours," Iris quipped, earning a shocked gasp from Mya. She certainly wasn't going to be having sex with Angelo. The very idea— A flash of heat and desire and longing unsettled her, but she hid it well under her annoyance with Iris for knowing her so damn well. "And might I add that Angelo isn't likely to stay this time, either. You'll give him your heart and he'll give you nothing in return. He'll leave."

"I'm not interested in marrying the man," Mya snapped, her temper rising. Iris held her ground and simply stared, her eyes hard. "Why are we arguing about this? I'm a grown woman. I can make my own decisions. I don't need anyone's permission. And maybe I want him to leave. Maybe I'm okay with sleeping with him and then watching as he goes on his merry way. Not that I'm saying I would or am…I'm just saying, I don't have to report to anyone about my personal life, and that includes you. I seem to remember I never judged you when you were going out and doing your thing back in the day. At least I'm not picking up strangers in a bar."

Iris blinked in wounded surprise and Mya realized she had been overly harsh. Immediately sorry, she reached out to Iris, but Iris wasn't having it and walked away but not before Mya caught the sheen of tears.

"Iris, wait…"

"Have fun doing whatever it is you're doing," Iris said, her voice husky with tears or pain, Mya wasn't sure, but she felt terrible for causing it. She shouldn't have said that. It was low and it'd taken a long time for Iris to come to the realization that what had happened to her hadn't been her fault. Miserable inside, Mya wanted to run after her friend, but she knew Iris wasn't going to accept her apology. Not yet anyway.

"Well, crap," she muttered, hating herself yet still preparing to meet Angelo. She grabbed her purse and closed up her office. "Here goes nothing...."

Darrick tossed in a sweat-soaked fever, the restraints on his arms and legs biting into his chafed skin. He was sober—a terrible consequence of getting locked up—but the nurse had given him some kind of drug that kept him locked in his own head, unable to get out.

And Darrick hated being in-his-head sober.

He had to talk to Angelo. Seeing the man after all this time, it had awakened something he'd have preferred to remain dormant—but he couldn't quite trust himself with the details. For all his alcohol abuse and subsequent vices, he knew he wasn't a well man and that sometimes what he thought he knew wasn't always true.

Except in this.

There was one thing he knew with the clarity of a man going before the Creator to be judged.

It was something he'd hidden a long time ago, back when he'd been terrified and alone. When Waylon had taken a bullet right in front of him. But he couldn't quite remember where he'd put it. It was definitely important, something he had to give to Angelo.

He groaned as his brain refused to cooperate, mushing the details of what he knew and what he thought he knew until the picture was fuzzy and distorted.

Darrick twisted against the restraint, as Waylon loomed before him. *Impossible,* he told himself, though he wasn't entirely sure, and it was the uncertainty that caused him to cry out in fear and pain. He thrashed harder and screamed, his throat convulsing on a ragged shout. The door opened, flooding the room with light, and a disapproving presence came into the room.

"Keep him here," the voice said as he shrank into the mattress, trying to get away. The disgust in the voice was clear. "His brain is pickled from all the drugs and alcohol. I don't know what else to do with him. What a waste."

The last part, muttered but crystal clear, made him want to tear off the restraints and rip out the man's throat, but he had neither the strength nor the courage.

Darrick stopped struggling and let the drugs steal his will to fight.

There was a reason he needed to wake up…but for the life of him, he couldn't seem to care.

Chapter 14

Angelo sat at his grandfather's old kitchen table that wobbled on uneven legs and nursed a soda. Grace always gave him a hard time for drinking soda when everyone else was slugging back beers or whiskey, but he never touched alcohol because of what he'd seen it do to the tribe. His own parents had been alcoholics and he wasn't about to tempt fate by pouring poison down his gullet for the sake of numbing what was happening in his head. He stilled when he heard a car come up the driveway. His heart rate kicked up, but he deliberately kept his seat and waited for her to knock. He'd given this night some thought as he'd waited. It was unlikely he'd get another chance to clear the air and although he might be a bastard, he was going to take it. Maybe it was selfish—okay, it was purely selfish—but he suspected Mya needed closure, too. And he owed her that, at the very least.

So if that meant he had to draw her to him under false pretenses, so be it.

A short rap on the front door sounded and, after a quick swallow of his soda, he rose and opened it with a sense of detachment. "I'd almost given up on you," he stated. She was only a half hour late but each minute had felt like an eternity. He'd almost been tempted to call her cell but he knew that would've put her in the power seat and he needed to be the one driving tonight. "That would've been fine but a call would've been professional," he chided her lightly.

She puffed up and lifted her chin, her eyes glittering coolly. "I'm here, aren't I? My world doesn't revolve around you, Angelo. I had business to attend to at the clinic before I came." She shrugged out of her coat and gestured to the table where he had his paperwork. "Shall we sit at the table?"

"Actually, my butt is numb from sitting in those hard chairs. Would you mind if we sat on the couch?"

She hesitated and was no doubt remembering the things they'd done on that very sofa so many years ago when his Papa had gone to run errands and Waylon had been off with Darrick doing God only knew what. He couldn't blame her. The memories had scorched him when he'd first walked through the front door. It seemed only fitting that she should suffer from them.

"It's not much to look at but it's comfortable enough," he said mildly, as if he thought that was her only concern.

She shrugged. "I'm sure it's fine. I was just thinking of the practicality."

"I'm good if you're good," he said.

Mya gave a minute shake of her head as if to say *whatever* and took a seat on the couch, but she couldn't have looked stiffer if someone had shoved a branch up her backside. She looked up to him, her eyes wary. "Well? Are we going to do this or stand around discussing the merits of an old sofa?"

He chuckled under his breath, scooped up his notes and stuck his pen behind his ear. "Thirsty? I've got some soda and bottled water in the kitchen."

"No, thank you," she answered, risking a glance around the small, shabby place. He caught sadness in her eyes before she could mask it, and he knew where her thoughts had traveled. It was hard not to remember Waylon and Papa. "It looks the same," she observed with a catch in her voice. "How'd you manage that? I would've thought everything would've disintegrated with time."

"I paid someone to come and keep the place up," he said, knowing his answer surprised her. He didn't blame her. He'd surprised himself when he'd set up the caretaker, but as much as he'd never wanted to return he couldn't let it molder into the ground. "He kept the place in order, with sheets on the furniture and whatnot."

"Why?" she asked, the bald question cutting at him. As if realizing she'd been rude, she rephrased it with more tact. "I know when Waylon and your grandfather died, you hated this place. I figured you would've been happy to see it fall."

"I couldn't," he admitted, adding with a slight arch to his brow, "Contrary to popular belief, I'm not that much of a bastard. I care about some things. Even old, smelly houses."

She let her gaze wander the old house, taking in the plank flooring that Papa had installed himself as a young buck with a family, and the rough-hewn table that Papa had fashioned from a fallen piece of cedar, to the rudimentary kitchen that surely wasn't going to win any awards but got the job done with a simple stove, sink and fridge. "It doesn't smell," she finally said with a tiny smile, the first since walking through the door. "I always liked it here. Your grandfather was a good man."

"Yes, he was." On that they could agree. Papa had been a very good man, solid in his beliefs, which were simple and to the point. Be good and Great Spirit will be good to you. Treat the land with the same respect you would your elder and take pride in who you are. But Angelo didn't want to talk about Papa. It was too painful. He grabbed his paperwork and shuffled through it, reaching to pluck his pen from behind his ear. "Has Bunny come to the clinic for treatment of the stomach problems he was talking about?" he asked.

Seemingly relieved that they were back on track, Mya shook her head, adding, "However, patient confidentiality prevents me from talking about any health concerns I've addressed with Bunny."

"I'm not asking for details, just confirmation or not," he retorted.

"I know what you're asking. And I'm telling you what I can within my limitations."

"Great," he said dryly. "Now that we have the fine print out of the way..."

"You didn't used to be so flippant," she observed, not shrinking or backing down from the look he gave her. He'd changed a lot since leaving the reservation. She was only seeing the tip of the iceberg. He remembered laughing more. Of course, back then, there'd been more to laugh about. The cases he handled, the people he dealt with on a regular basis and the job itself had a tendency to leach the joy out of his life. He shrugged off the weight of her stare and her judgment, intent on returning to the case, but she wasn't finished. "I remember a different you. I know we all change and sometimes change is a good thing, but I don't know you well enough any longer to say whether this is a good change or not."

It wasn't. He couldn't say that he'd improved since bailing on his people, on her. Damn. How'd she manage to turn the tables on him so quickly? He shot her a cool look. "What happened to no talk of us? Because if you want to go there, I can with no qualms. I've got things to say and I suspect you've got plenty to say to me." He finished by affecting a lounging position against the cushion, watching and waiting for her next move. She regarded him with those fathomless dark eyes, and, though he wore an armor of confidence, his insides had begun to shiver at the very real fear that whatever she had to say, he didn't have the strength to hear.

Mya felt played. She could sense a world of deception in that gaze of his, and she didn't buy his nonchalance one bit. One thing she remembered about Angelo was that he had always been a cool bluffer. He'd stood down bullies twice his size without flinching because he'd carried himself with the strength of a much bigger man. Later, he'd confide in her, joking that he'd been scared spitless and had been hoping and praying that he didn't end up a smear on the pavement.

She smiled, enjoying the slight falter in his smirk. Anger, fresh and raw, gave her smile an edge, she could feel it. He had no idea what he was playing with and she certainly didn't appreciate his easy treatment of their past. "You wear arrogance well," she said softly.

"But I think you're lying. You're not so jaded that you don't feel something since coming home. The thing is, I think it's because of what you feel that you're deliberately acting like an idiot, because if people are angry with you then they stop asking the questions you don't want to answer."

"Very philosophical. What would you say if I told you that the whole reason I asked you here was to get you into bed?"

She laughed. "Nice. Another attempt to deflect, but here's the rub, earlier I said I didn't know you any longer, but that's not true. Standing here now, watching you try to pull off this act, it's readily apparent that in some things you haven't changed at all." He stiffened, and she continued, almost smugly. "I know your tricks. You can't bluff me. And so I have to ask why you're going to so much trouble to color my opinion of you. What are you afraid of?"

"Who says I'm bluffing?"

Mya held his gaze, felt the pull between them and heard Iris's voice in her head screeching at her to stop, but the man was mesmerizing to look at. She understood attraction, knew the physiological signals, and even accepted that it was likely she was sinking to her basest levels of human nature, but then she'd be the one dissembling. She couldn't hide behind clinical explanations when her heart was hammering in her chest and her body was heating simply from sitting near him. The attraction was there, alive and well and demanding attention. *Back down, don't go there.* His tongue slid along his bottom lip and he started to lean toward her, his gaze feasting on her mouth. But just as her breath hitched in her throat, caught between desire and prudence, she managed to scoot away, putting a safe distance between them, saying with only a slight shake to her voice, "I came here to help you with your notes. So let's get to that, shall we?"

Angelo's nostrils flared at her rejection, and she might've seen a hint of relief mixed with disappointment, which she understood because she felt the same. He relaxed again, chuckling as he grabbed his pen. "I bet you drive the guys crazy here."

"What do you mean?" she asked, not sure she wanted to hear the answer.

"Forget it." She pinned him with a hard look that communicated how she felt about those types of games and he relented. "Well, guys love a contradiction. You're all professional with the doctor gig and you wear it well. But all a guy has to do is look past the uptight persona to see the wild woman beneath. You are sex and erotic fantasies tightly locked down behind that serious nature. You used to be a lot less…locked down. But that's okay. Guys love that. So I'm sure you're a real treat here on the rez."

"If you refuse to act like a grown-up, I'm leaving. I didn't come here to talk about my sex life. I came here to help, but I see that's not what you had in mind." She rose and she saw surprise in his eyes, as if he hadn't expected her reaction. "Tomorrow I'll meet you at Bunny's, say, around 10:00 a.m.? I'm bringing Iris and Sundance with me, so keep your inappropriate comments to yourself or risk an unpleasant altercation with my brother."

"Mya, wait," he called after her, but she was already walking toward the door. In truth, though her words were stern enough, deep disappointment was etched on her heart. She was nearly to the door when Angelo reached out to grasp her arm, his touch scorching a gasp from her. He let go but in his eyes she saw regret deep enough to drown in. He appeared vulnerable, nothing like the man who'd taunted her with blatant sexual suggestion. That man she wanted nothing to do with, but the man standing before her was a different matter entirely. "I'm sorry," he said. "I was out of line. I don't know what came over me. I truly would appreciate your help. Will you stay?"

Mya considered his request. She ought to leave to prove her point. But she felt that might be an overreaction. He'd apologized. And it had been sincere. "I'm willing to help you, Angelo," she said. "But there are certain areas you are not allowed to trespass on. You lost that right a long time ago and I don't see that changing any time soon. Are we clear?"

Angelo's shoulders sagged minutely, as if her admission was a bleak confirmation of something he'd already suspected, but he nodded with a humble plea that nearly broke her resolve. "Please stay."

Self-preservation urged her to leave. But in truth, she craved his touch, the smell of his skin, the low timbre of his laughter when it was lodged deep in his chest. She missed him so much sometimes she wondered if she'd ever get past the fact that they weren't meant for one another. It felt like a physical ache that refused to subside no matter how hard she tried to rub it out.

"I'll stay," she said, even though she knew she was making a huge mistake—one that could cost far more than her heart could afford.

Chapter 15

Angelo's heart thudded painfully and his mouth filled with a bitter taste. He'd been stupid to play mind games with Mya. She'd always been smarter than that and he was ashamed even to have tried it. At some point he'd lost control of the situation, going from the teacher to the student, and Mya had plainly schooled him. Secretly, he was glad she'd called him on it. Again, her strength amazed him.

She settled on the couch and he did the same, only this time, he was all business, which helped him to focus.

"What do you remember about the day Waylon died?" he asked, trying to stay removed from the emotional trauma of losing his little brother by coming at the case as he would that of a stranger.

She seemed to understand his need for distance. "You and I were here when the call came in. You were helping your grandfather outside and I was making a pot of beans for you guys to eat later that night."

"Papa always loved your beans," he murmured, remembering. She smiled briefly at that. "And then we went and identified the body because we were worried about Papa's heart not being able to take the strain."

She nodded, her eyes sad.

"Waylon and Darrick were going to catch crawdads to go with the beans for dinner. I remember he'd been going to the river a lot with Darrick but I didn't think much of it, because what kind of trouble could he get into on the river?"

"You couldn't have known. We'd all spent our childhoods on that river," she said. "Speaking of, Darrick was brought into the clinic the other night. He was a drunken mess, not that that's new, but he was really agitated. He kept saying that it was his fault Waylon died. Do you know why he might say that?"

Angelo frowned, shaking his head. "What happened to Darrick? After I left?"

Mya's mouth turned down in faint distress. "He really went downhill. Alcohol and drugs became his life. He does odd jobs on the reservation, but for the most part he lives down by the river. He has a tent he stays in and people bring him blankets and food at times so he doesn't freeze or starve."

"What about his big-shot father?" Angelo asked, remembering Darrick's father, Randy Willets, was one of the few tribal members who didn't live from check to check, having made his money in investments off the reservation. "He still around?"

"Oh, yes. Randy is very involved with the flood relocation efforts. He's taken a special interest in the Hoh

River. He monitors the flow and tracks the levels for the tribe."

"Must be hard to have your only son turn out that way," he murmured. He had never thought much of Randy Willets. For some reason, he always felt that the man was looking down his nose at Waylon and Angelo because of their parents. Sometimes he wondered if Darrick's original motivation for befriending Waylon hadn't sprung from the boy's desire to thumb his nose at his father in any way he could. "Has he disowned Darrick or something?"

"No. He bails him out of jail sometimes or gives him money for food. But the two have never gotten along. I think Darrick would rather starve than accept much of anything from his father. It's a sad situation aggravated by some sense of guilt Darrick is carrying over Waylon."

"But why would Darrick blame himself? As I remember, Darrick loved Waylon like a brother."

She nodded. "That's what I remember, too. But you know, something must be eating at Darrick because he was never the same after Waylon died."

He'd known Darrick had taken Waylon's death hard, but so had every person who'd known him. His little brother had been loved by everyone. Waylon had had a way about him, charisma, he supposed. Something Angelo apparently hadn't been blessed with. But it did seem odd that Darrick was blaming himself for something that had clearly not been his fault. Or was there more to the story than they knew?

"Where's Darrick now?"

"We had to send him to the mental health facility in Forks. He was combative and we don't have the resources to house someone with Darrick's specialized needs."

"Can he have visitors?"

"I suppose. Are you thinking of seeing him?"

"Maybe. I don't know," he mused, mulling it over. "Or maybe I'll pay a visit to his father first. If Darrick's mind is as compromised as you say it is, it might be a wasted trip. His father might know something, though."

She agreed. "He's fairly easy to find. Just pop into the Tribal Center tomorrow, he'll be there because it's flooding season." Mya cracked a yawn as she rubbed her eyes. "I think I'll call it a night," she announced. "I hope this helped."

"It did."

Mya offered a somber smile as she said, "I miss Waylon. He was a great kid."

He nodded, no argument there. "As little brothers went he was pretty good, too. I wish I'd been a better older brother."

"You were a great big brother," she said, a spark returning to her eyes.

He was flattered that the spark was born of the need to defend him, but he knew the truth. He'd utterly failed as a brother, caring more about himself than what was happening around him, particularly when it concerned his annoying baby brother. "If I'd known that day was going to be the last…I'd have kept him from going to the river. I'd have done a lot of things differently."

"I don't think it would've mattered. It was his time. Great Spirit collected him for reasons we aren't privileged to know."

She was trying to console him, but he didn't share the tribal beliefs and the words only served to make him uncomfortable. "Well, screw that. I would do anything to bring him back. He deserved a life."

Mya's dark eyes filled with sorrow. "White Arrow," she said, shocking him with the use of his tribal name. "There's a hole in your soul, punched there by something and left unhealed. Maybe you need to journey. You know, Porter has an extra spot on his team for the canoe journey. I think it'd be good for you to connect with your ancestors."

He withheld a groan of irritation. But as he started to say something flippant, he saw genuine concern in her eyes and it tempered his tongue. There was a time when he'd had the privilege of her care and concern every day. In deference to those times, he jerked a short nod. "I'll think about it," he lied.

"Your grandfather used to take that journey, didn't he?" she asked, though she knew the answer. She just wanted him to remember that fact. He supposed Mya wasn't above emotional manipulation, either.

"Yeah. He always wanted us to do it. Waylon was signed up to participate the year he died. He never got the chance." Angelo stopped, a memory breaking loose of a newly hulled cedar canoe tipped upside down in the shed out back. Good God, it was probably sawdust by now. "Did Porter carve his own canoe?"

"No, I think he purchased it, but it's a good one. Solid."

He didn't know why he asked. It wasn't as if he cared, but he didn't want Mya to leave and talking about canoes seemed a safe enough subject—until he realized it was likely Mya would remember the one Papa had been carving for Waylon. "How is Porter?" he asked, remembering the man from their youth. They were all about the same age though they hadn't been buddies.

She skirted her gaze away from his and shrugged in answer. "Real good. He works for the tribal office. He does important things for the tribe. He's a good man," she added, almost defensively.

It was the odd note in her tone that snagged his attention. That coupled with her body language told a story. "You and him an item?" he asked.

"We dated a short time but it's over now."

The wild thrill that arced through him was troublesome enough, but the ribbon of possession that tightened on his feelings about Mya gave him pause. Of course she was free to date whomever she pleased. So why did the idea fill him with misery?

Mya knew she ought to leave. The hour was late and way past the point she'd told herself she'd stay. Except, she couldn't quite bring herself to go.

The darkness blanketed everything outside, and the sounds of night creatures echoed from the shadows. Mya felt cocooned in a place that wasn't quite real and she desperately wanted to remain, if only for a little while longer.

She had missed this—talking with a man who'd been her best friend. But it was far more complicated than that, even. Iris was the sister of her soul, but what she'd had with Angelo had transcended friendship and even being lovers. It was a fusion of both relationships and that's what she'd missed. It was this desperate longing that pushed her to stay when she knew that she ought to leave.

A featherlight touch at her temple startled her but she leaned imperceptibly toward it. Her eyes drifted closed, and she savored the quiet moment between them. It had been a long time since she'd lost herself in the pleasure of a man's touch. She and Porter had had sex but she'd always kept herself apart at some level. Sometimes, it had felt clinical because her brain never truly shut off to just enjoy the act. For that reason, she'd started to pull away from Porter, using work duties as an easy excuse.

And it had worked. She'd pretty much sealed off the valve controlling her sexual side, which had been a relief.

But now, here with Angelo, all those buried needs and desires rose like a wave inside her, obliterating all the good reasons why it was important to keep her distance.

Don't say anything, she prayed silently. *Just touch me.*

Angelo seemed to know her mind and the chaotic place she was caught in. His hands moved to the column of her neck, caressing the heated skin, drawing her to him. The press of his lips against hers nearly broke her. An answering shudder moved through her body and she opened her mouth to receive the touch of his tongue.

Sweetness unfolded from his sure hand, obliterating the fear and uncertainty with the rightness of the moment. He was different from the boy she'd known, but what was familiar in him called to the memory of what they'd once shared and she eagerly followed.

Angelo tried to stop. He knew this was a mistake but his hands seemed to have a mind of their own as they roved Mya's body, delighting in the silky texture, the dips and curves unique to her. Her breasts fitted perfectly in his palms, and would fit even better in his mouth.

He was still fully clothed, the only remnant of his good judgment, but his erection strained to be free, pressing painfully against his zipper as he ground against her, wanting desperately to feel skin on skin instead of this teenage groping session hampered by fabric. Her breasts, freed from her bra, begged for attention, and he couldn't resist.

The minute his mouth closed over the pebbled nipple, her gasp sent a thrill down his vertebrae, ringing a bell, pressing a button—whatever you want to call it—it unleashed a fury of barely restrained desire to rip every shred of clothing hiding her treasures from him. He wanted to taste every inch, revel in every discovery.

Was it because at one time they'd been innocent together? Something primal and dangerous growled in his heart at the idea of anyone else doing what he was doing to her. He pushed that feeling away and focused on the physical pleasure of the moment.

She groaned, twisted beneath him, wrapping her legs around his trunk, pulling him tighter to her hot core. He sucked harder, drawing that tight bud into his mouth, swirling the tip with his tongue, laving it with dedicated attention to every detail. Her clever hands darted straight to his erection and rubbed the length, causing sweat to pop along his hairline.

Stop before it's too late, a voice cautioned, but it was already too late. He'd put a bullet through anyone who came between him and Mya at this moment. His hands, urgent and shaking, divested his body of all clothing while she did the same.

Naked, their bodies collided, rubbing and moving in all the right spots. Spots danced before his eyes as her hands ignited a firestorm everywhere she touched.

He pressed fervent kisses down her trembling stomach, loving the way the dim light illuminated the peach fuzz along her body, giving her curves a soft glow. Her scent called to him, evoking a memory buried deep. It was Mya, everything he remembered about her, all his fantasies. Her hands caressed his head as he bent to taste her in her most secret spot. Mya inhaled sharply as his tongue delved between her folds, seeking and finding the swollen little nub that, when coaxed with a knowing hand, would drive her crazy. He recalled from memory what she liked, driving her mercilessly toward that pinnacle. Her breathing quickened, her whole body tensed as her legs began to shake and a cry erupted from her throat as she went limp. He rained soft kisses along her hipbone as the waves of her climax continued to rock her body. Her cheeks were flushed and her lips red and plump, while her head lolled to the side as she tried to catch her breath. The corners of her mouth tipped in a shy smile but it was the carnal message in her eyes that stole the air from his lungs and froze him in place.

But not for long.

He lunged at her and she flipped onto her belly with a laugh. He was rewarded with the most beautiful view of her heart-shaped behind. He covered her with his body, his rock-hard and aching erection prodding at the cleft of her cheeks as he whispered into her ear the things he wanted to do to her. Playfulness gone, she moaned and arched against him in invitation. "Less talk, more action," she gasped even as he lifted her hips toward him. He'd never seen anyone so beautiful. The old sofa creaked under their weight, but otherwise the only sounds were soft moans and pants as he teased her with the head of his erection.

When he finally plunged inside her, she was nearly growling at him with frustration.

The tight fit, the overall rightness shot him straight into oblivion and he lost his mind, pumping into her sheath with hard intensity, wrenching another orgasm from her just as his own climax drained him of everything he had and then some. *Good God.* He'd never known such pleasure.

He collapsed against her, his heart beating so swiftly he feared a heart attack, but he didn't care. Peace unlike anything he'd ever remembered settled in his bones, turning him to jelly.

He had the wherewithal to pull out of her but they were both spent and not going far. Wordlessly he grabbed the blanket he'd given to Grace that first night and covered them. She snuggled against him like a spoon in a drawer and they both fell into a deep, sexually sated sleep.

But not before Angelo heard that voice again.

There's no walking away this time....

Chapter 16

Morning afters were so awkward—and this one was no exception.

Mya awoke alone on the sofa, naked under the blanket she'd shared with Angelo. She wrapped herself up and gathered her clothes from the floor. Angelo appeared from the kitchen, showered and dressed even though it couldn't have been 6:00 a.m. yet. He held a coffee cup in each hand.

"I figured coffee was a safe bet…" he said, lifting a mug and gesturing to the kitchen. "Or do you want to shower first?"

She felt incredibly awkward standing there naked as a jaybird, nothing but an old blanket covering her while Angelo looked ready to go to work. There was nothing of the sweetness she'd seen last night, and his general air of perfunctory politeness was enough to send her running to her car in shame. But she wouldn't. She lifted her chin, determined to appear as unaffected as he was. "I think a shower would be best," she answered.

"First door on your right," he supplied as if she didn't remember where the damn bathroom was in a house where she'd spent practically every waking hour of her youth. "Sorry I don't have any fancy soaps or lotions," he said, sipping his coffee. "But I didn't figure I'd be having company aside from Grace, and she's not big on that sort of thing."

"Whatever you have will be fine," she said, turning and making her way to the bathroom, her temper rising with each footfall. Did he really think he was handling the situation with any sort of finesse? They were both adults, they could admit that the situation was awkward without succumbing to cliché behavior. He certainly didn't need to treat her like some stranger he'd picked up in a bar that he couldn't wait to get rid of. Her cheeks burned at his dismissive tone. Well, she'd brought it upon herself, hadn't she? It wasn't as if he'd started spouting poetry and singing ballads about their lost love. It had been about physical need, nothing more.

She wrenched the tap and moved out of the way as water came pouring down from the showerhead. Stepping into the spray she let the water sluice over her, pelting her with almost painful force. *Calm down,* she told herself. *Get focused.* She refused to be that woman people pitied because she'd read more into a physical act than it warranted and had ended up crying over the rejection.

So they'd had sex. So what? Mya scrubbed at the prickling in her eyes, hating that she'd wanted it to mean more to him than it obviously had. How could he fail to notice how his hands had trembled when he touched her? How they'd both lost all sense of reality in each other's arms? She stifled a growl of frustration—both with herself and the situation—and stepped from the shower to towel off. Fine. He could kiss her—

"Mya…"

Angelo's urgent voice at the door halted her mental diatribe. "Yeah?" she called out, tucking the towel tighter around her. "What's wrong?"

"Sundance just called. Something's happened to Bunny. Ambulance is en route to the clinic."

He didn't need to tell her that they had to get moving. She hustled into her clothes, still half-wet and sticking to the fabric. "I'll be out in a flash," she said, throwing her wet hair into a messy bun. She opened the door and Angelo stared for a moment, as if stunned. He swallowed and in a blink of an eye he became once again the man who'd casually mentioned she could shower if she chose. No cuddling, no snuggling—just polite disinterest.

She moved past him, thankful for something else to focus on aside from the mess they'd made of things. Great Spirit help her, Iris had been right. Good thing they hadn't placed money on that wager. She'd be lighter in the pocketbook.

Mya shrugged into her coat. "Any details?"

"Bunny's been shot. Sundance said he thought we ought to know seeing as we were planning on returning to his place today to question him."

"Oh, my God." She nodded. "Let's go then."

"I'll follow you," he said, grabbing his keys.

They both climbed into their respective cars and within minutes they were driving toward the clinic. It seemed dangerously coincidental that the minute they started asking questions about a case that obviously had Bunny and Hettie jittery, Bunny ended up hurt. She just hoped it was simply that—coincidence—but she held on to the hope with the weakest grip. Bad things were circling the reservation. She could feel them.

Angelo cursed himself for being a randy idiot, letting his hormones and unresolved issues take control of his actions last night. He'd tried his best to appear as if he weren't questioning every decision he'd made since stepping foot on the reservation again but it was hard to ignore the facts. The minute he'd seen Mya, the emotions had nearly swamped him. If it had been difficult to remain focused with only the distant memory of their time together, now it would be downright impossible. Everything was fresh and real in his head. He could still smell her on his skin.

Lying there with Mya tucked against him it had been easy to slip into an illusion of happiness, to forget that they were worlds apart in their beliefs and compatibility. Being good in bed together wasn't a recipe for relationship success. Neither was being on separate ends of the spectrum when it came to loyalty. Mya was stubbornly loyal to the tribe, whereas he felt nothing.

A memory burst forth of Waylon, right before he died. The kid had been so proud of that damn canoe. He'd been sanding it with Papa, next they were going to paint it. Waylon had been wiping it down, ensuring that the wood was clean and smooth and free from any remaining sawdust.

"Why are you doing this?" Angelo had scoffed, earning a scowl from Waylon.

"Why wouldn't I? I'm proud of my heritage."

Angelo thought of the poverty that went hand in hand with the rampant alcoholism on the reservation and he didn't see a proud people. He saw a broken remnant of what had once been a strong tribe. Why celebrate the tribe's failure to survive and adapt?

"Paddling a canoe across the peninsula isn't going to put you in touch with your ancestors," he'd told Waylon. "It's a waste of time."

"To you. Just because you refuse to care doesn't mean I can't."

Angelo remembered the proud, defiant tilt of his brother's chin, the way his eyes flashed with indignation at his dismissal, and for a moment Angelo wondered where that fire in Waylon's heart came from when his own heart felt cold. For a quick, disconcerting moment he'd desperately wished he felt the same as Waylon, that tribal pride pulsed in his veins in the same hot, vibrant way as it did for his brother. But it didn't. At least not anymore. Maybe once it had. Before their parents had died. But where had Great Spirit been when their car had careened off the Pititchu Bridge and straight into a tree? Where had their ancestors been when their parents had started drinking and never stopped?

And where had Great Spirit been when someone put a bullet through his little brother's back?

If he ever felt the stirrings of tribal pride, it was answerless questions like those that snuffed out any flame that might have sparked to life.

And he doubted there was anything that would ever change that fact.

Mya hurried through the side door of the urgent care facility, Angelo on her heels. She caught sight of Iris running by with a packet of blood and foreboding followed. The commotion of the emergency room narrowed her focus. Dr. Frederich Solvang, her replacement, worked quickly to stem the blood that seemed to pour from Bunny's wound like water through a holed bucket. She stayed out of the way and gestured for Angelo to do the same. She could sense his impatience, his frustration, but he held back.

It seemed an age before Dr. Solvang muttered an expletive and resignedly called Bunny's time of death.

Angelo swore under his breath, and Mya held back her tears. He'd been alive only yesterday. She turned away. It wasn't that she was squeamish around death, it was that she couldn't escape the feeling that they'd caused this to happen somehow.

"I need to speak with Hettie," Angelo said in a low tone as they put some distance between themselves and the body.

"I think she's in the lobby. Let me speak to her first," Mya said, worried over how unstable Hettie was going to be with the death of her husband. They'd fought like cats and dogs but, deep down, they were twined together in a codependent knot, and without him she might unravel. Angelo seemed reluctant but nodded. She found Hettie nervously rocking in her chair, a tissue clenched in her hand. She looked up when Mya appeared and with one glance, Hettie knew Bunny was dead. "Hettie—" Mya began gently but was interrupted by a low, keening sound that tore at Mya's heart.

"My Bunny…he's dead, isn't he?"

She nodded sorrowfully, moving to sit closer to the older woman. "What happened?" she asked.

Hettie shook her head, unable to speak. Mya soothed her, but caught sight of Sundance and Angelo heading for the distraught woman. She sighed and moved away, going to Sundance. "She's pretty upset. I doubt she'll be able to answer your questions."

Sundance nodded. "I'll have to try just the same.

Details are fresh in her mind right now," he said, going to Hettie. Angelo kept a respectable distance but Mya could tell it was killing him.

"Where was Bunny when he was shot?" Sundance asked.

"He was outside by the woodpile. I told him not to leave for the river before hauling me some logs for the woodstove." She wiped at her running nose. "I can't lift them anymore and my arthritis acts up in the cold so Bunny always made sure I had wood for the day before he went fishing. And then I heard a shot."

The statement drove home how close the two had been, even if the face they presented to the world had been antagonistic.

"Who would've wanted to hurt Bunny?" Sundance asked gently, to which Hettie jerked her head in an agitated movement. "Was someone angry with him?"

Hettie pursed her lips but the tears started to flow again and Mya felt her brother's frustration. She moved in, giving Sundance a gentle nudge. She gave Hettie a fresh tissue and tried a different tack. "Does this have something to do with the sore on Bunny's arm?" she asked quietly.

Hettie blew her nose loudly, taking a long moment to answer and when she did, there was fear in her rheumy eyes. "They were going to kill him one way or another," she whispered. "Just like that agent…just like little Waylon."

Chapter 17

Every muscle in Angelo's body was strung taut. He fought the need to shake the answers out of the old woman, knowing it would only cause her to clam up even more.

He'd heard every word but the one that scraped like a hot razor across raw skin was his brother's name. Everything came back to Waylon. Damn, what had his little brother been mixed up in? How could Angelo have been so ignorant? So blind to what was happening beneath his nose?

Sundance helped Hettie to her feet and out the door of the clinic and Mya came toward Angelo, her expression grim. "Sundance is going to take Hettie to stay with her niece for the time being. She doesn't feel safe at her place, not that I blame her." She wrapped her arms around herself, shuddering. "This is getting scary. There's no way we can pretend that bad luck was involved with the deaths, including Waylon's."

"I agree," he said darkly. "I'm wracking my brain trying to remember what Waylon had been into back then. But I was too self-absorbed and worried about what was going on in my own life to worry about my little brother."

Mya frowned in thought, then said, "Darrick was Waylon's best friend. If anyone would know what was going on, it would be him."

"Yeah, but I thought you said his brain is pickled? Would he even remember?"

"I don't know. It's worth a shot, right?"

At this point what other choice did he have? He was chasing a ghost. And ghosts rarely gave up their secrets without prodding.

Angelo excused himself to call Grace.

"Miss me already?" she quipped dryly as she answered on the first ring. "What's up?"

"People are dropping like flies here on the reservation," he grumbled, a frown creasing his forehead. "So much for low profile. When are you coming back?"

Suddenly serious, Grace's voice lowered. "What's going on?"

"Bunny Roberts, a man who ran the bait shop on the river, was killed. We were going to talk to him regarding my brother's death when he was shot in the head about a half hour ago. Clean shot even though the sun had just begun to rise and the light was milky. Had to be done by someone with skill."

"He got any enemies?"

"He was a cantankerous old man but everyone seemed to tolerate him fairly well. I mean, I can't imagine that anyone was so angry with him that they'd pop his head off. No…this is related to the cases we're working. He knew something. For that matter, his wife, Hettie, knows something, too, but she's clammed up tighter than a drum because she's afraid she's next if she opens up."

"She might be right," Grace said. "Listen, I can't cut out of here for a few more days. And I don't like you going all John Wayne—pardon me, Crazy Horse—on your own. Maybe we ought to turn this case over to another team. It's probably time anyway."

He smirked, but there was nothing light in his heart as he said, "When have I ever done things the way they ought to be done?"

"Never."

"No sense in starting now. No one is going to take this case from me. It's personal."

"Exactly. You're losing your objectivity."

"Give me a few more days. Can you run interference with the director for me?"

"I suppose," Grace said, her tone worried. "Just don't get yourself killed, all right? I don't want to train another partner."

He smiled. "I'll do my best not to inconvenience you with something like my death," he joked, but he knew she was concerned. Grace had been bounced from one partner to the next until she'd landed with Angelo three years ago. The two oddballs had been a good fit. "I'll keep in touch."

"You'd better," she said. "All right, chase after this, but I swear, if you put my ass in a sling…"

"It won't come to that. I'm going to stop whatever the hell is going on here. That's a promise," he said quietly. There was no stronger sense of conviction than what he felt right now. Someone had messed with his family long ago and now it was payback. Plain and simple. And even if the Bureau saw fit to pull him from this case, he wasn't going to stop.

Maybe that's what Hicks had felt. That driving force, compelling him to keep digging while his efforts were taking him closer to a sinkhole that would swallow him whole.

So be it.

There was one thing he had that Hicks hadn't—tribal knowledge. He knew the people, their ways and their weaknesses as well as their strengths.

And he wasn't above using any and every advantage, even if it wasn't fighting fair.

His gaze went to Mya—beautiful, strong, unattainable—and quite possibly the means to solving the case.

Time to make amends.

Mya had bigger things to consider than her own wounded ego, which was why when Angelo came to her for help connecting with Randy Willets about his son, Darrick, she placed her bruised feelings aside. There'd be a reckoning later, but she'd built her adult life on pushing away that moment. What was another item added to the list?

"Are you okay?" she asked Angelo as they drove to the Tribal Center where Randy volunteered during the spring. She'd accepted Angelo's offer to drive since it seemed silly to tail each other all over the place, but now that she was sitting close enough to see the texture of his skin and smell the sharp, clean scent of his deodorant, she wished she'd politely declined. She was only human. Even as she tried to keep her mind on task, memories of last night assaulted her without mercy—so much so that her palms had begun to sweat and her body temperature was climbing. Realizing Angelo hadn't answered, she looked to him curiously. "Care to share what's going on behind that faint scowl?"

"This case...everything. It's hard being back again."

"I can imagine," she murmured, though it was difficult to truly understand what he was going through and she knew it. But if anyone had an inkling, she did. She curled her fingers into her palm, resisting the ridiculous urge to smooth away the lines in his face. That wasn't her place, nor would he welcome it. Ah, crud. There rose those wounded feelings again. She pulled her gaze away from him to stare out the window.

"Has Randy Willets changed much over the years?" Angelo asked, returning the conversation to the case. "I remember him being a bit of a snob, always looking down his nose at everyone. I can't imagine why he stayed here, especially after what happened with his son."

"He's not that bad. Maybe old age has softened him a bit," Mya offered, shrugging. "I've never had a problem with him. He comes into the clinic for his annual check-ups and he's always friendly."

"That's because you became a doctor."

"And you became an FBI agent. I'd say we both did pretty well for ourselves."

He grunted in response and she smiled. Angelo still wore his feelings on his sleeve, even if he tried to hide them. Funny how he thought Randy was the snob. Growing up, people had thought Angelo was the one always looking with disdain at everyone.

Angelo let that one go and said, "Tell me again what he does for the tribe."

"Well, each year the flooding has become worse, destroying houses and eating away at tribal land. We've been trying to make a case for an acquisition of more land in the Olympic National Forest but the wheels of government move slowly. Randy has been tracking the river's flow and movement for us, documenting it each year with measurements and erosion comparisons so the Council has hard data to make our presentation."

"Why the interest?" Angelo asked.

"What do you mean?"

"No one does something for nothing. What's his angle? There has to be something in it for him."

She stared at him, irritated. "Not everyone has an ulterior motive aside from kindness and altruism."

His expression said he didn't believe that for a minute and her anger turned to sadness. Angelo lived in a world where nothing was taken at face value and he was trained to catch evidence of lying and deceit, just as she was trained to catch signs of disease or sickness. But it had made him hard inside. She longed to reach inside him and caress that cement lump that was his heart and mold it into something that could beat freely again. Her fingers fluttered in agitation as she shook off her thoughts and simply shrugged in deference to Angelo's cynicism. "Believe what you want. Just try to be sensitive when you question him. His only son is… well, certainly not the man he'd hoped he'd turn out to be."

"Yeah, well, that's life," Angelo muttered. "At least he has his son. My little brother, Hicks, Bunny…they're never coming back."

She fell silent. There wasn't much she could say to that. It was true.

They pulled up to the Tribal Center, a brand-new building nestled among the Western hemlock, red cedar and silver fir, built with grant money up and away from the flood plain. It still smelled of fresh lumber and paint, its newness representing everything that was possible for the tribe in the future. At least that's how Mya chose to look at it. She wondered what Angelo saw. When he'd left the reservation, there hadn't been much in the way of new beginnings. She hoped he saw how things were slowly changing.

They walked into the Tribal Center, greeted by a gorgeous mural painted on the wall by a local talent, and he stood stunned for a moment. "This is pretty amazing," he murmured. She seized the opportunity to brag a little.

"This was done by a high-school student, Sierra Buck," she said, smiling with pride.

"A kid did this?"

"Well, she started it in her senior year and finished it before she went to college. It was therapeutic for her."

He looked at her sharply. "What do you mean?"

"She'd been attacked by the same serial rapist who attacked Iris. This mural was part of her healing journey."

Angelo digested the information, and just when she thought his silence meant he wasn't interested in anything unless it pertained to the case, he asked, "Is she okay? The girl?"

"She is still healing emotionally but she's doing quite well in college. She's majoring in criminal law. She wants to make a difference in the world and we're all very proud of her."

He nodded, and it was as if the information was both a relief and a burden to him. He moved away and gestured to get back on track. "Where can we find Randy?"

Mya withheld a private sigh. Well, she wasn't sure what she'd expected. It wasn't as if he was going to suddenly see what he'd refused to see for as long as he was a resident on the reservation. She pointed to the office directly in front of them. Angelo nodded and walked briskly to the closed door. He rapped twice and then strode inside.

No polite waiting for an invitation to enter, no awaiting someone else's convenience.

A smile found its way to Mya's lips. He still hadn't learned the value of simple tact or persuasion. In some ways, he was much like Sundance.

She followed and the smile remained, only she let Angelo assume the smile was directed toward Randy.

Let the man think what he wanted.

Her grandmother used to tell her, a woman needn't always reveal the secrets of her heart.

And her grandmother had been a very wise woman.

Chapter 18

Randy Willets looked nearly the same as Angelo remembered from his youth, only now the older man's stomach hung low over his beaded belt buckle and the buttons on his expensive shirt strained to keep his girth contained.

Randy's brows rose in surprise. "Angelo Tucker? Is that you?" Angelo nodded in answer and Randy stiffened imperceptibly. "What are you doing here? I thought when you left you weren't coming back." He shot a look at the man he had been talking to, which Angelo capitalized on, extending his hand to the stranger.

"Sorry to disappoint you," he said to Randy but looking straight at the other man. "Special Agent Angelo Tucker, actually. And you are…?"

The man, roughly the same age as Randy and dressed with a sharper sense of style, accepted the handshake, but there was a wariness to his stare as he answered, "Joseph Reynolds. A pleasure."

"Joseph is my cousin and business partner and he was just leaving," Randy said curtly.

"Cousin? I don't remember you...did you grow up on the reservation or elsewhere?" Angelo asked, curious.

"Second cousins and no, I grew up in Seattle, but I visited the reservation in my youth. Beautiful place."

"Yes," Angelo said, then added with a shrug, "Well, that is, when people aren't being picked off like flies. Have you heard about that?"

Joseph shifted and shared a look with Randy before returning to Angelo with faint interest. "Yes, I've heard there's been some unfortunate circumstances. Are you investigating?"

"I am."

"Good luck. I hope you find what you're looking for," he said, then turned to Randy, saying, "I'll be in touch."

Angelo moved aside so Joseph could leave and after a long moment he returned his attention to Randy, who looked very unsettled. "It's hard to do business with family. At least that's what I've heard. You seem tense. Everything all right?"

"Your concern is touching. What can I do for you?" Randy asked, not budging an inch and quite obviously not in a sharing mood. Fine by Angelo.

"Well, as I mentioned to your cousin, I'm investigating the death of a federal agent who died on Hoh soil."

Randy grunted and leaned back in his chair, his eyes remaining cold. He flicked his gaze to Mya, finally acknowledging her presence. "Nice to see you, Mya."

"Hello, Randy," she said with a nice smile, no doubt

trying to smooth over the rough edges between him and Randy. "I know you're busy with the flood data, but we need to talk to you about Darrick."

Randy frowned. "What about him? He done something?"

"I heard he's in a mental health facility, his brain messed up from drugs and alcohol," Angelo said, not pulling any punches.

Randy's mouth thinned. "Is that why you've come? To rub in my face how my son turned out? Does that give you some kind of pleasure?"

"No," Angelo answered. "It wasn't Darrick's fault you were his father."

"You always were a little prick," Randy growled, causing Mya to interject with a sharp look thrown Angelo's way.

"Randy, let's put aside old grudges for now. The agent who was killed here was actually investigating Waylon's death, and, as you know, Darrick and Waylon were very close when they were kids. We wondered if you might remember anything the boys were into that might give Angelo some insight as to who might have had a reason to hurt Waylon."

At the mention of Waylon, Randy's shoulders sagged just a little. It was a subtle movement but Angelo caught it. The fact that Randy felt anything for Waylon surprised him. He'd always looked down on his son's friendship with "that Tucker boy," as he'd called him. In fact, he'd probably been the only person on the reservation who hadn't had a soft spot for Waylon.

"Darrick and I didn't have that kind of relationship. He didn't share his private business with me," Randy said, looking away. Was that guilt in his eyes for quitting on his son at such an early juncture in his life? Or was it something else? Randy cleared his throat as if something were caught in it and said, "Anyway, Waylon's death was long ago. Nobody should start poking around. Let sleeping dogs lie."

"That sleeping dog was my brother."

"I didn't mean it like that," Randy said. "Waylon was a good kid."

"Funny, that's not how you felt back when he was alive."

Randy met Angelo's hard stare without flinching. "People make mistakes. Even me."

"Gentlemen," Mya interjected firmly, determined to keep the conversation steered in the right direction. Angelo caught her look of irritation and heard Grace's admonition in his head. Damn, he *was* losing objectivity. He needed to get his head on straight if he wanted to remain on the case. "Three people are dead. We need to find out who is committing these terrible crimes so Angelo can stop them. Randy, we need any help you can give us."

Angelo swallowed his ire and jerked a short nod. "Mya is right. Whoever killed Waylon is likely responsible for killing Agent Hicks and Bunny Roberts. Someone is going to great lengths to make sure something stays buried."

"Maybe," Randy allowed, shifting in his chair. "But I don't know what Darrick has to do with it. He's incapable of even feeding himself these days. I doubt he'd be able to kill someone."

"He might know something," Mya said. "He seems to feel a certain amount of guilt over Waylon's death. When he was in the clinic the other night he kept saying that it was his fault that Waylon was dead. Do you know why Darrick would feel guilty?"

"They were best friends," Randy muttered. "I imagine losing your best buddy like that at such a young age… I don't know. Like I said, Darrick and I have never been close. Whatever he's feeling, he hasn't shared with me."

Angelo swore silently. He'd hoped for some kind of lead, some kind of direction. He fished a business card from his pocket and handed it to Randy. "If you think of anything, give me a call."

Randy accepted the card, but Angelo was betting it landed in the trash as soon as the door closed behind them.

Mya thanked Randy for his time and Angelo left her to the niceties. When she emerged from the building, her frown spoke volumes. "Did you have to be so antagonistic?" she asked. "You're not going to get far with that kind of attitude and you know it. So why are you acting like this? Don't you want cooperation?"

"Of course I do," he answered, a bit surly only because he knew she was right. He choked down his bad attitude. It wasn't Mya's fault that he had issues with the tribe that dug beneath his skin. "I'm sorry, I lost my head a bit in there."

"You know, Randy's been through a lot with Darrick. It's been a constant struggle since Waylon died. Can you imagine how disappointed and hurt Randy must feel to bear that burden?"

"No heavier than the burden of a dead brother," Angelo quipped and was immediately sorry. He was doing it again. He shoved his hand through his hair, wondering when he'd lost control of his mouth. To her credit, Mya simply waited out his bad temper. She looked gorgeous, standing there with a no-nonsense expression that should've looked stern and austere, but he saw only strength shining in those brown eyes. It was no wonder she bore the weight of the tribe so easily. If anyone should have been chief, it was Mya. He was seized by the desire to pull her into his arms, to feel that lean body pressed against his, to shelter her against the bitter chill that came from the river. But that would only serve to confuse them both, so he kept his hands to himself. "Looks like a trip to see Darrick is next. You up for a short drive?"

"I'm ready when you are."

She smiled and he nearly stumbled from the shock to his heart. How amazing would it be to have her love again? To have the privilege of waking up beside her every day? To earn the right to call her his woman? A melancholy pain spread through his chest when he realized he'd have better luck wishing on a star than dreaming about a future with Mya.

He'd efficiently severed that tie long ago. Clean and brutal. He had no right to hope for anything but what she was giving right now.

So get focused.

"What do you know about this Joseph Reynolds guy?" he asked.

She shrugged. "I've only met him a handful of times but he seems like your average business-type person. To my knowledge Randy and Joseph started their textile business in Seattle and they've been fairly successful. That's where Randy made his money. He stayed on the reservation to take care of his parents while Joseph oversaw the day-to-day at the plant."

"They seemed to be having a disagreement when we walked in."

Mya nodded. "Randy's face was flushed. He ought to be careful of his blood pressure. I've been after him to take better care of himself. Probably something business-related. The economy has been tough on everyone these days. He shared with me that his company had taken a big hit in the last year because of all the outsourcing to India for textiles." She sighed, as if feeling sorry for Randy and his troubles. "Anyway, I get the sense that Randy and Joseph have always butted heads but they remain tied to the business. I doubt they're close, even if they're related."

Angelo tucked that piece of information away for later and returned to the situation at hand.

Mya had to question what she was doing. She should've given Angelo directions to the mental health facility and then returned to work, but knowing the clinic was in good hands lessened her urgency and freed her to make decisions that were probably unhealthy in the long run.

The truth was, she enjoyed spending time with Angelo. After all the years they'd been apart, she would have thought that the feelings she'd had for the man would have turned to ash a long time ago, but that wasn't the case. Having sex with him certainly hadn't helped. Iris had been right. Perhaps her feelings for Angelo weren't quite dead after all. She thought of Porter and how unfair she'd been to allow him to think they had more of a connection than they did. She must've sighed because Angelo turned and called her on it.

"You okay?"

She nodded, not quite sure she was ready to have that conversation with Angelo.

"I'm sorry I overreacted with Randy," he said, staring back at the road. "You know, when I was a kid, I was constantly trying to outrun the reputation of my parents as no-good losers. It's like no one could look past their actions and see me and Waylon for the individuals we were. It's what I hated most about this place."

"Angelo, not everyone saw you and Waylon that way," she said gently, remembering Angelo's struggle. "Your grandfather was a very good man. People respected him as an elder. It was unfortunate that your parents were trapped in the vicious cycle of alcoholism that so many of our tribe fell into. But you were not judged and neither was Waylon."

He disagreed, shaking his head sharply. "No. Randy Willets always looked down his nose at us. He never liked Waylon and Darrick's friendship for the simple reason that we didn't have money."

"Randy Willets was a snob back then. He's changed," she said. "I think watching your own flesh and blood disintegrate changes you. He'd probably do anything to be able to make different decisions that would change how everything turned out. He has his own demons, too."

Angelo let that statement sit between them for a long moment until he grudgingly saw her point. "Yeah, I suppose we'd all make different choices if given the chance."

She couldn't resist and it was selfish of her but she asked, "Even you?"

He didn't hesitate. "Of course. Isn't it obvious?"

The breath seemed to catch in her chest and she struggled to remain impassive on the outside when inside her heart had begun to beat erratically. "Nothing is ever obvious with you. You left without warning. I'd had no clue you were thinking of abandoning us all."

"Mya, I'd been telling you I wanted to leave for months. That I was miserable here. You're the one who didn't want to leave, so I figured it was best to cut ties before it became too painful for us both. I figured you'd marry and have kids and leave my memory far behind. I wanted you to, actually. I didn't want you to eventually resent me for not sharing your love for the reservation."

She tried not to let it but the memory of that morning came crashing back. Her nose tingled as tears filled her eyes. She blinked them back, determined not to cry in front of Angelo. "You didn't give me the chance to make that decision. Maybe I would've left with you."

He shrugged. "Maybe. I wasn't in a good place emotionally. I was really angry and bitter. I wouldn't have been a good partner. Eventually you would've left and resented me anyway."

"It wasn't your place to make my decision for me," she said stiffly, hating that the mere mention of that time broke her calm. Her hands drifted to her belly before she realized it with a start and resolutely crossed her arms across her chest. "It doesn't matter, it's in the past. Let's stay focused on the present."

"I'm sorry, Mya," he said, his tone truly apologetic. She risked catching his gaze. There was sadness and regret in those eyes—and it didn't help her resolve. "I was a young kid, hot-blooded and angry, not the best combination. I should've given you the chance to come with me."

She choked back the rising lump in her throat. How many years had she longed to hear those words? Too many. And now? What did it mean? Nothing. They were simply words meant to soothe an old injury. She jerked a nod, wishing he'd stop talking. Silence was infinitely better than this soul-searching. But instead, her own traitorous mouth started talking, revealing too much. "I had something to tell you," she said, barely able to hold back the tears. "Something important."

"When?"

"The day you left," she admitted, remembering. "I found your note and I thought you were just blowing off steam. I never imagined that you would disappear."

Angelo looked shamed. "I thought about calling, to let you know where'd I be, but it seemed less painful to deliver a clean cut."

A clean cut? That's what he felt he'd delivered? Hardly. It'd felt as though someone had sawed off her limb with a dull blade. But that pain had been paltry in comparison to the agony that would follow shortly after.

"Tell me now," he said, trying to make amends, but he had no idea what he was trying to heal. "I want to know."

"It's over and done. I don't really want to dredge it up."

"Please."

That plea nudged her in the wrong direction. Her bottom lip had begun to quiver and a tear slipped down her cheek before she could stop it. Alarmed, he reached out to her but she jerked away. "Mya," he said, concerned. "I have to know, what were you going to tell me? Something is eating at you and the least I can do is try to make amends here, now. I'm listening."

"It's silly that I'm still so affected by it," she said, wiping at her tears with ill-disguised disgust with herself. "I mean, it was so long ago. But each time I get near the memory, I crumble. It's… I don't know, maybe I need therapy."

Angelo pulled onto the shoulder and put the car in Park. He turned to her and pinned her with that dark gaze so that even if she'd tried she couldn't get away from his intense stare. "Did someone hurt you?" he demanded, jumping to the wrong conclusion. A near hysterical laugh bubbled out of her throat, further confusing him. "Mya?"

This was it. She had to tell him. Fifteen years was a long time to carry her pain alone, but she had never imagined this was the way it would come out, with her sitting across from him, holding back a nervous breakdown, while they were on a trip to talk to a crazy man. He said her name again, only this time with more urgency, his eyes turning black from the conclusions he was drawing. She crumpled, dropping her face into her hands, unable to look at him a moment longer. "I was pregnant. I was going to tell you that I was pregnant."

Chapter 19

Angelo stared, unable to comprehend what Mya had just said. "What do you mean?" he asked dumbly, and she lifted her head to regard him with red-rimmed eyes and cheeks streaked with tears. He regretted the stupid question, but he couldn't quite wrap his head around her admission. His mind quickly put the remaining pieces together. "What happened?"

She swallowed and wiped at her cheeks with her sleeve. "I miscarried at thirteen weeks."

Sadness swamped him for a child he'd never known existed, for the brief window his baby had been alive. He pushed against the steering wheel with locked arms, resting his head against the headrest, not quite able to process the bomb Mya had dropped.

"I wanted to tell you. I was going to tell you, but your grandfather had just died and I was waiting for the right moment. I wanted it to be happy news, but then the morning I made the decision to tell you, I discovered you'd gone."

"And I hadn't left you a contact number to find me," he said in a low voice, more than ever hating the decision he'd made. "What happened then?"

She sighed, a sad little sound if he'd ever heard one. "Well, I figured I would raise the baby on my own. Just when I'd come to grips with the situation, I awoke spotting. A sonogram revealed the baby's heart had stopped beating and I was miscarrying." She stopped for a minute to collect herself, then admitted, "The news broke me. I didn't have you and I didn't have the baby anymore. It took a long time to get over and some days, I don't know if I am over it."

"I'm so sorry," he said. "I should've been there for you."

"Yes. You should have," she whispered, not letting him off the hook, and he didn't blame her. He was only feeling a fraction of what she must have gone through. She took a halting breath before continuing. "I kept thinking you would contact me and let me know where you were, but it was as if you dropped off the face of the planet. It took a long time before I stopped hoping every time the phone rang that it was you. I needed a distraction and I needed space. I put myself through college at Oregon State and then went into med school. Once I finished my residency, I came back here and I've been here since."

"I thought I was doing the right thing," he murmured, angry at the situation. "I thought... Well, it doesn't matter what I thought, does it?"

She offered a sad smile. "It doesn't do any good to beat yourself up over it now. It happened. It was a long time ago. I've moved on."

He couldn't resist. He leaned over and drew her to him. She went without resistance, her lips soft against his. "I would've been there for you," he murmured against her mouth, hating that he'd been the source of her tears and that she'd gone through something so painful alone. "I'm so sorry."

He pulled away and the shine in her eyes nearly undid him. A trail of moisture snaked its way down her cheek and he wiped it away with care. What could he say that would make this better? Nothing. He knew that, but he desperately wanted to offer something to show that he understood how deeply he'd messed up. But words failed him and he could only hope she knew in her heart.

"We should get going. Visiting hours will be over soon," she said quietly, dragging him back to the moment and their true purpose.

"Yeah, I suppose you're right. I just don't know how to act like I don't know that you were once pregnant with my child. It's heavy stuff. How do you move on from that?"

"When I figure that out, I'll let you know," she said wryly, a spark of humor showing through. He took heart in that and followed her lead.

Mya thought she might be in a mild state of shock after unloading her private pain on Angelo. Of course, it was appropriate to unload on him since her ordeal had involved him, but she couldn't quite believe she'd finally been able to tell him. She'd imagined all sorts of scenarios, but none had been close to the reality. Oddly, she felt relieved. For so long, she'd carried around the secret of her miscarriage—only Sundance and Iris had known—and now she felt as if she could actually move on.

The rest of the trip was filled with light banter, almost as if they were simply on a drive rather than going for any specific purpose, but as they arrived at the mental health facility, the seriousness of the situation settled over them and they grew silent.

The austere building wasn't much to look at, with very little landscaping to break up the institutional aspect of the place. "Cozy," Angelo said, taking it in. "Well, let's get this over with, shall we?"

That's precisely the way she felt, too. She knew Darrick's mental state was precarious at best, and there was no telling how he'd take to seeing Waylon's brother. It might actually throw him into some kind of psychotic episode. Mya shuddered and pulled her coat more tightly around her. "Remember, he's not very coherent most times. Don't take it personally if he says something outlandish or rude. He doesn't know what he's talking about most of the time."

He nodded and they entered the building. After Mya handled the paperwork, they were taken to Darrick's room.

Darrick was housed in a small room, with padded walls for his safety, and he was tied with restraints. It tore at her heart to see just how far Darrick had fallen. She remembered him as a boy. He'd been a good kid, always prone to laughter, with an infectious guffaw that had seemed to come from his toes. He hadn't been terribly handsome but there'd been a boyish cuteness to him that might have matured into attractive adulthood; but the ravages of his alcohol and drug abuse had taken that possibility from him. His head was shaved—something they'd done when they'd brought him in—and his face had red, raw scratches, probably caused by his own fingernails.

"Damn," Angelo said under his breath, earning an I-told-you look from Mya. *Here goes nothing,* he thought as they closed the door behind them.

He approached the bed with caution, keeping Mya behind him. He needn't have worried, he realized as he got a better look at the man. Disappointment welled inside him. "He's doped to within an inch of his life. He's no more capable of answering questions than a turnip." He muttered a litany of curse words. Mya stepped forward to check his pupils and his pulse. She frowned. "What's wrong?" he asked.

"He's way too sedated," she murmured with concern. "His heart rate is incredibly slow and sluggish. I'm going to get an orderly. I want to see his chart."

She disappeared with the swift and sure stride of a woman in charge, and he took the opportunity to take a closer look at the man, trying to find a remnant of the boy he'd known.

He remembered Darrick having thick wavy black hair that was always fashionably trimmed, while Waylon had preferred his hair long and wild. Darrick had called his brother a hippie. A faint smile touched his mouth as he remembered their heated arguments over stuff that didn't matter in the big scheme of things, except to teenage boys who thought it had meant everything. Darrick's skin was sallow and sagging beneath the once-healthy tan of their tribe; a ribbon of drool escaped his slack mouth where his gums revealed a few missing teeth, and the teeth that remained in his head were completely rotten. Unexpected tears sprang to Angelo's eyes as he stared at the ruin of the man he'd known as a boy. What would Waylon have done for his friend? Would Darrick have turned out better if Waylon had lived?

Mya returned with an orderly, her expression stern. "I want to know whose signature this is," she said to the orderly, who looked annoyed but mildly worried at Mya's authoritative tone. "This man is clearly over-medicated. He needs immediate medical attention."

The orderly stared at the chart, his mouth pursing, until he slowly shook his head. "Well, it says Dr. Overton, but he left for the day. It couldn't be him." He looked at Mya, swallowing as if he were afraid he was going to get fired for the mistake. "I don't know who signed this," he admitted. "But I didn't administer the meds, that's the nurse's job. Want me to get him?"

"Please," Mya said crisply, returning to Darrick's side to do another check. "And get the on-call doctor. Immediately."

The orderly disappeared, only too happy to escape Mya's flashing eyes and disapproving stare. Mya in action was a sight to behold. And he was a total pervert to find this side of her completely arousing. He shifted, hating that neither his mind nor his body seemed to behave appropriately given the situation. He was grateful when Mya gave him something else to focus on.

Mya looked to him, worried. "Angelo...I think someone has tried to kill Darrick and make it look like an accident. The man is barely breathing. If we don't get him to a hospital, he might die."

"Who'd want to kill Darrick?" he asked.

"Someone who wanted to keep him quiet. Someone is afraid he'll tell something he knows."

Angelo's mouth firmed. That was sure as hell not going to happen. Even if it meant he had to stand guard over Darrick's door all night. "What do you need to do to get him out of here?" he asked.

"Technically, he's under the state's care for the moment. We'd need his father's consent to move him."

"Not if he just became a federal witness," he said. "Let me make a call."

Angelo stepped outside the room, ignoring the curious looks from the orderlies who'd no doubt heard about the mix-up and were wondering who was going to catch hell for it, and dialed Grace. True to form, she picked up almost immediately.

"What's up?" she asked, no-nonsense as usual.

"I need to put a guard on a possible witness and I want it to be you."

"I'm flattered and annoyed. Since when did I sign up for babysitting duty?"

"Someone's tried to kill Darrick Willets. Something tells me it's because he knows something that someone wants to keep quiet. It needs to be you because you're one of the few people I trust."

"Stop, I'm getting misty," she quipped, quoting one of her favorite Mel Gibson movies. But she relented with a snort. "You owe me. Big-time. I don't do babysitting details unless it's the President."

"Yeah, I know, you're a badass," he said dryly. "When can you be here?"

"Lucky for you my detail here is finished. I can be there in about an hour. Think you can handle things until then?"

"Yeah, I think I can handle it."

"See you in a few, then."

The line clicked off without ceremony—no mushy sentimental stuff from Grace. He appreciated her style. He wished he could go back to that, especially when it came to Mya. It would simplify things by half because then their interaction would just be about the case. But that wasn't his reality. He was burdened by the knowledge that she'd briefly carried his child, that if fate had been less cruel, or he'd been less stupid, he'd be a father right now to a fifteen-year-old child. Would he have had a son? Or a daughter? A lump rose in his throat and he swallowed it down with difficulty. *Focus, Angelo. Now is not the time.*

He returned to find Mya sitting by Darrick's bedside, having hooked him to a machine that monitored his vital signs. "No one knows who authorized this medication and no one saw who administered it," she said crossly. "This is unacceptable in a facility like this. If we hadn't stopped in, Darrick's heart would've stopped beating."

"It couldn't have been an innocent mistake?" he asked, wanting to make sure they weren't overreacting, though he already knew the answer.

"No. The amount given to him does not match the amount written on the chart. It's clearly an overdose."

He nodded, confident in Mya's skills. He tried to keep the pride from his voice—but he was damn impressed—as he said, "My partner Grace is on her way back. She's going to stand guard over Darrick's room until he comes to. She'll make sure that no one gets near him unless I clear it."

"Sounds good," Mya approved. "In the meantime, I want him transferred out of this facility and into a real hospital. Forks Community Hospital has agreed to take him. The ambulance is on the way now." She leaned back in her chair, clearly troubled. "You know, I feel bad."

"Why?"

"Well, not only did I send him here, but I can't help

but remember all those times I've treated Darrick in the recent past, ignoring his ravings as those of a man suffering from extreme intoxication. He might have been trying to tell me something this whole time."

"You couldn't have known. Anyone else would've treated him the same."

"I should've tried harder to listen. I feel I've watched as one of our own drowned."

He went to her and touched her shoulder—it was the only place he'd allow himself to touch—and tried to reassure her. He hated to see her carry the entire weight of the tribe on her shoulders. That should have been his job. "We're listening now," he said.

She rewarded him with a smile that zeroed in on his heart, piercing it with unerring accuracy. "You're a good man, Angelo," she said with complete conviction.

He gave her a crooked grin, knowing he wasn't deserving of such unfettered praise. "Don't go making snap judgments," he warned with mock seriousness. "I'd hate to prove you wrong."

Mya gazed at him without guile and said without reservation, "You won't."

Angelo thought his heart would stop beating.

To have Mya in his life was something he could only dream of.

It certainly wasn't something he deserved.

Mya needed someone strong in their beliefs, someone who shared her love of their heritage—someone who didn't carry the stain he wore for walking away from everything, everyone that had ever mattered.

He knew this, knew it with the certainty of a brand on his skin, and yet, he yearned to be the person who deserved her love.

But he also knew that some things weren't meant to be, no matter how hard you might wish for them.

Because that was reality.

Chapter 20

Mya liked Angelo's rough, army-strong partner with her close-cropped hair and U.S. Marine build. She had the kind of personality that made a wardrobe of combat boots and barbed-wire tattoos look completely appropriate, and yet she had kind eyes that shone with intelligence and insight. Mya could see right away why Grace got along so well with Angelo. It also made Mya ridiculously relieved to know that Grace and Angelo shared absolutely no romantic chemistry in the least.

Grace walked into Forks Community where Darrick had been transferred and assessed the situation with frank objectivity. "This drooling mess is who I'm guarding?" she asked.

"Yes," Mya answered. "At least he's an alive, drooling mess, which he wouldn't have been if we hadn't shown up. I talked with the medical staff and no one could vouch for the nurse who'd administered the overdose. Someone came in disguised as a nurse and then took off after dosing Darrick. An orderly found a balled-up pair of scrubs in the trash outside the loading dock."

Grace looked to Angelo. "You send it off for processing?"

"Of course. Maybe we'll get lucky and get a hit on some DNA left behind."

Grace shrugged. "Anything could happen, but I wouldn't pin your hopes on it."

"That's what I love about you—your eternal optimism," Angelo said, causing Mya to smile.

"That or my effervescent charm," Grace quipped right back, adding a deadpan "I'm sweet enough to cause cavities. Back to the case, though. What's the story with this guy?"

"He's a local character who may know something about who killed Waylon back in the day. They'd been best friends at the time and joined at the hip. Not to mention, he's never been right since Waylon died."

"Guilt, perhaps?" Grace surmised.

"That's what we're thinking," Angelo agreed. "And it's important to keep him alive so he can tell us who might be trying to kill him and why."

"The problem is that he's not completely coherent even when he's not doped up. He's done a lot of damage with the drug abuse."

Grace nodded, understanding softening her rigid stance. "Poor bastard," she murmured, then straightened. "I'll keep him safe. You can count on me."

Angelo smiled. "I knew I could. That's why it had to be you."

"I'll call as soon as he's awake or if anything else happens," Grace said, all business.

"I've informed the medical staff of your involvement. Whatever you need, don't hesitate to ask," Mya said.

Grace nodded and they filed from the room, where Grace remained stationed at the door and Angelo and Mya went outside to get some fresh air.

"You know, I was thinking, we could work in shifts," Mya suggested, not liking the idea of leaving Grace to red-eye the night. "I don't mind."

"Grace is in her element. Trust me. No, I think we ought to get a hotel room, get some sleep, that way we'll be fresh when Grace calls."

A silent thrill chased his words but she focused on keeping her expression neutral. He was likely being practical, not romantic, which was the way it should be. A pinch of guilt followed when she recognized disappointment at the idea of spending the night together for purely sensible reasons, yet she nodded resolutely. "That's smart. There's an Econolodge just up the road from the hospital. I saw it when we came in."

Angelo nodded, and while he went to tell Grace their plan, Mya took a private moment to quell the butterflies in her stomach and the intense yearning she felt to be cocooned in Angelo's arms, safe and removed from the confusion of the moment.

Mya bit her lip as the voice of reason filtered through her thoughts, reminding her sharply that she was being a silly, lovestruck fool. One night was a drop in the bucket compared to a lifetime of misery if she continued to harbor these fruitless feelings for a man who had not only left her once, but had no intention of staying the second time.

And so it was pointless to pine for a man whose future was on a different path from hers. Wasn't that one of the reasons she hadn't gotten serious with Porter?

Good, sweet, dependable Porter? Because she couldn't imagine a future spent across the breakfast table from a man who had a tendency to slurp when he ate his cereal and who bored her to tears on road trips because he insisted on listening to political radio instead of music? And yet, here she was getting dreamy-eyed over a man who was uncommunicative, obsessive, moody and carrying more baggage than a Boeing 747. *Yes,* she answered herself, her breath catching in her throat as Angelo emerged from the facility, his sharp-angled features a gift from his ancestors and most certainly the kind of stuff that made women look twice if they passed in the street.

She smiled as they walked wordlessly to the car. An easy silence floated between them—as if they were accustomed to each other's presence and comfortable with the space they inhabited with one another—and as they went off to find food, Mya accepted the stark truth staring her in the face.

If tonight were to be the only time with him, she'd take it—even knowing that his leaving would hurt just as much as it had the first time and his departure would likely leave an even bigger hole. She didn't care because she wanted to soak up every minute with Angelo. She wanted to feel his skin against hers, taste the sweat on his body and brand her soul with his touch—this way, she reasoned, when he left the second time, she'd have fresh memories to visit when the sadness and grief washed over her.

Iris would say she was nuts. Maybe she was. All she knew was that tonight would end the way she wanted it to.

Even if Angelo didn't know it yet.

* * *

Angelo tried to tell himself that a hotel room was simply more sensible than driving all the way back to the reservation, but all it took was one look from those smoldering brown eyes to know that to cling to such an obvious lie was an exercise in futility.

He wanted her. Plain and simple.

Except there was nothing simple about it.

If sleeping together the other night was a bad call, what was doing it a second time? He knew the answer but it wasn't going to matter.

The knowledge that Grace was standing guard over Darrick freed his mind to wander, to propose all kinds of sultry and sinful acts he wanted to do to Mya. Was he a bastard for wanting her so desperately, for going after her with the single-minded focus he usually reserved for chasing criminals? What was in it for Mya, aside from a good romp in the sack? She deserved better than that—particularly from him—but even that didn't stop him from pushing open that hotel door and eagerly following her inside, practically tripping over himself in his haste.

His heart rate was so elevated he thought he might have some kind of cardiac event. As soon as the door opened and Mya saw the single king-size bed, he held his breath, waiting for her to object, but she simply put her purse on the small bedside table and announced she was going to use the bathroom.

Just like that…as if this was completely normal. He sat on the edge of the bed, waiting, not quite sure what the hell they were doing—what they were doing to each other.

Mya wasn't the sort to have a short-term, no-strings-attached love affair. And he wasn't in the market for a soul-stirring, emotional cataclysm. But he wanted her with a ferocity that shook him.

He scrubbed his hands over his face and fell back onto the bed. "This is lunacy," he muttered to himself. There was no way he could go through with this knowing he wasn't offering her anything beyond the physical. He wasn't that big a jerk. It was bad enough he'd abandoned her when she'd needed him the most. An ache that had nothing to do with sexual need spread through his gut. He'd do anything to go back in time to rewrite that single moment. She hadn't deserved that kind of pain. She'd never been anything but good to him. Angelo ground his eyes with the flats of his palms, a heavy sigh escaping as he prepared to be a gentleman and keep his hands to himself.

The door opened and he sat up only to stare at Mya framed in the doorway, wearing nothing but the skin Creator had given her.

"Wha— *Mya!*" How could he follow through with the gentleman act when she was standing there like an Indian princess, teasing him with everything he shouldn't touch? "Wh-what are you doing?" he asked, trying his damndest to affect a stern tone, but it was difficult to pull off when all the spit had deserted his mouth, making speech nearly impossible.

She walked toward him, her eyes shining in the dim light, a hungry smile on her lips. She straddled him and his arms instinctively wrapped around her lithe body. The heat of her core seemed to sear through his pants, urging him to divest himself of the barrier between them. She pressed little, sweet kisses along his jawline, rubbing her beautiful, perfect breasts against his chest, and uttered a low, throaty laugh when he palmed the soft, plump flesh of her behind. He groaned, trying to remember why he wasn't going to do this, but he was only human and she felt like heaven in his arms.

"Are you sure about this?" he managed to ask, his voice shallow and raspy as she plucked the buttons from his shirt, spreading it open to bare his chest and shoulders to her view. She nodded in answer, more intent on his body than on his attempts to keep them both from doing something they might regret later. "It's probably not a—"

"Shhh." She placed her fingers against his lips, following the soft admonition with a drugging kiss. *What the hell?* he thought muzzily, allowing her to push him to a prone position with her on top. *Let's do this...*

He rolled her to her back, pinning her to the bed with his body. She grinned and wrapped her legs around his trunk. His erection strained against his zipper, demanding to be sprung. He liked to think of himself as an elegant lover in most circumstances, but at the moment he had about as much finesse as a man with six thumbs. It took every ounce of willpower to slow himself down and take his time. Her skin, soft and sweet, tasted like fine wine on his tongue. He delighted in the soft cries she made as he teased each nipple in his mouth, playing and sucking, nipping and laving. And when he reached down between her curls he found her slick and ready, so he slid a finger, followed by another, rubbing the spots that he knew drove her wild.

He withdrew his fingers and quickly shucked off his pants, but before he could plunge inside her, she turned the tables on him and her hot, wet mouth was on him, sucking greedily, gripping him to her with strong fingers.

He groaned, his hands buried in her hair, nearly delirious with pleasure as Mya tortured him with her clever mouth. He couldn't take any more without fear of exploding, and he didn't want things to end like that. He wanted to come inside her, to feel her clench her body all around him. He pulled away and climbed onto her body, fitting himself to her hot core. She gasped as he slowly slid inside, burying himself deep.

"Oh, God," he said tightly, the words wrenched from his mouth. Everything felt right, felt so good. He drove into her body with ruthless abandon, losing himself to the sensation, to the wild sounds of their lovemaking, and as he came, he dimly wondered how on earth he thought he could live without this woman when she turned his heart inside out and teased his body to a fever pitch with a touch.

Collapsing, he rolled to his back, panting from the exertion, and it was a long moment before either could speak.

The sweat glistened on their bodies, the low light from the single bedside lamp caressing the hills and valleys of Mya's body, and even as scattered as his thoughts were after a mind-blowing orgasm, he realized Mya was quite possibly the most gorgeous woman on earth.

And once, he'd been blessed enough to call her his own.

Could she love him again? After all this time? After all she'd been through at his hands?

It was a cruel fantasy—one he pushed away before it started to sting too badly. He just wanted to enjoy the moment.

Was that too much to ask?

Hell, yes.

But he was going to do it anyway.

Chapter 21

Mya rested on her side, gazing at Angelo while he slept. She loved this man. Perhaps she'd never stopped loving him. Was that why she'd failed to find another man to fill the hole he'd left behind? Was it possible to watch him leave without dying inside? She sighed softly and the sound caused Angelo's eyelids to flutter.

A sleepy smile followed and he instinctively reached for her, fitting her to him so that her bare breasts tickled his chest. She rested her leg over his and they locked together like puzzle pieces.

"I've been very irresponsible with you," she admitted in a husky whisper. The sleep cleared from his gaze and she smoothed the gathering frown from his face. "But I can't seem to help myself."

He remained quiet for a moment, then he nodded. "Me, too."

She smiled. "I don't mean just sexually. I mean emotionally, too."

"I know."

He felt the same? She tackled the first issue because somehow, it was easier. "I'm not in the habit of falling into bed with people. Usually, I require a full medical work-up before I decide to get physical with someone. And I always use a condom."

"A full medical work-up," he repeated, his tone faintly amused. "Sounds romantic."

"It isn't, but it's necessary these days," she said. "However, I wanted to assure you that I'm on the pill so there's no worries there." She expected him to sigh in relief, since they'd overlooked that detail in their lust-induced haze, but instead she saw something else flicker in his gaze. "Angelo? You're relieved, right?"

He pulled away, his expression openly conflicted. "I should be."

"You're not?" she asked, confused. "I don't understand."

"Me, neither," he admitted, rolling onto his back to stare at the ceiling. "I don't know, Mya. My head's still not screwed on straight after what you told me yesterday." He returned to his side to gently palm her belly, making the breath catch in her throat at his reverent touch. "When I think that our baby had been here...I..."

She blinked back sudden tears. She understood how he felt, but she was shocked that he was feeling it now, too. "It was for the best," she said, nearly choking on the sentiment because, although she trusted in Great Spirit's guidance, she still couldn't understand why her child hadn't been given the gift of life. "Neither of us was ready to be a parent."

He nodded as if he agreed, but the pinch of his mouth

told a different story. "You would make a wonderful mother," he said softly, following his hand with his mouth, pressing a sweet kiss on her belly. "Strong. Resilient. Kind." He punctuated each word with a kiss. "A mother who would shape fine sons and smart, capable daughters."

"And what about you? What kind of father would you make?" she asked, barely able to speak.

He met her gaze and she saw so much pain she wanted to cry out. "I doubt I'll ever have the chance to find out."

"Angelo," she whispered, pulling him to her. "You will. And when you do, you'll be an amazing father who is kind yet firm, loving and supportive because that's what Papa taught you about being a man."

"What if I turn out like my father?"

"You don't even drink. It's hard to turn into an alcoholic when you don't touch a drop of liquor," she answered, smiling through a wash of tears. "Don't let a ghost influence your decisions for the future. You're more like Papa than you let yourself remember. Someday... you'll remember and everything will fall into place."

He buried his face against her skin, as if hiding from the world, and she gladly sheltered him.

In a blinding moment of clarity she realized she wished she'd been off the pill so that perhaps she and Angelo could tempt fate twice, but that was a selfish yearning, born to breed heartache and she knew she couldn't do that. But it didn't stop her from being a little sad at what would never be.

Grace called as they were checking out of the hotel.

"He's awake—sort of. You might want to get down here," she said, her tone ominous.

"What's going on?" Angelo asked, shrugging into his coat and heading for the car with Mya in tow.

"Well, the drug he'd been given caused some kind of reaction in his already failing liver. He crashed early this morning and he's not doing so good. Any questions you might need to ask him…you're running out of time to ask them."

Angelo pursed his mouth in agitation and frustration. "We're on our way." He clicked off and met Mya's wide-eyed stare of concern. "Darrick crashed this morning. The drug affected his damaged liver… he's in bad shape."

"Oh, God, I was worried about that," she said. "Poor Darrick. I hope he can pull through, not just for the case, but because I want to help him get into a rehab facility."

"Yeah, me, too," he said. He'd even pay for it if he had to. It seemed the least he could do to make amends.

They walked into the hospital and met Grace in the lobby. "He was finally pulling out of the drug-induced stupor and just as he started to breathe on his own, he began convulsing," Grace explained, shaking her head. "I'm not sure he's going to pull out of this."

"He has to," Angelo said, feeling as if his one true chance at getting answers was dying along with Darrick. "Damn it," he muttered.

"His liver was teetering on the edge of acute failure before the drug overdose," Mya said. "It's a wonder he's lasted this long with the kind of abuse he's subjected his body to." She laid a hand on his back, her touch gentle. "We'll figure something out. I promise."

He nodded, wishing he had Mya's determined optimism. Right now, he felt as if he was back to square one with very little to show for his efforts aside from a head and heart warring with one another.

A doctor emerged, wearing a solemn expression. Angelo knew, just as Mya did, that the news wasn't good.

"Are you friends of Mr. Willets?" he asked.

Mya stepped forward, extending a hand. "I'm Dr. Mya Jonson. I'm the one who had Darrick transferred here from the mental health facility where he'd been given an overdose of sedative. This is special agent Angelo Tucker and his partner, Grace Kelly. What is the prognosis?"

"Not good," he admitted with a heavy sigh. "I wouldn't say that it's impossible, as miracles happen, but his liver is far too damaged to sustain that kind of blow. If you'd like to see him, to pay your respects, I'd advise you to do it now. But I should warn you, it's unlikely he'll even know you're there."

"Thank you, Doctor," she murmured, glancing at Angelo, who nodded his appreciation for the doctor's attention, then he and Mya went into Darrick's room. Machines keeping the man alive beeped and hissed, while the smells of death and sickness floated on the cold, sterile hospital air. Angelo hated hospitals. They reminded him of all the people he'd lost in his life: his parents, Waylon, Papa. Hospitals were a place of sadness and despair. Today was no different.

They flanked Darrick's bedside, each nearly at a loss for words. A pall had settled on the room as if the specter of death was hovering at the foot of Darrick's bed, waiting for his moment to collect the troubled man's soul. Angelo's throat closed and he wished Waylon were here. It shouldn't end like this. Hadn't the tribe suffered enough? As he stared at the ravaged face of Darrick Willets, he wondered if he could have made a difference if he'd stuck around, maybe taken the kid under his wing when Waylon had died. He'd been so damn selfish, only thinking of himself and acting on his deeply entrenched anger against everyone and everything when, in fact, he'd been angry with himself for not rising to everyone's expectations, especially those of his loved ones.

He was supposed to be the tribal chief—the last of his line. He'd thrown it all away. Damn, he was drowning in regrets. He looked to Mya, whose focus remained on Darrick. Compassion softened her expression and his heart contracted. Her heart was big enough to encompass the entire tribe, yet she'd given it to him exclusively.

And he'd stomped on it.

Was there any way to make amends for that kind of injustice? He didn't know, but he wanted to find out.

Mya knew Darrick was struggling to hold on; she'd seen enough instances in the emergency room when a patient clung to life against all odds. Darrick was a fighter, even if his body wanted to give out on him. However, she also knew his strength would only last so long before his body simply lost its grip on the rope tethering him to this world.

She wanted to console Angelo. He looked broken, almost as if Darrick's decline were his fault, when, in fact, Darrick had been actively trying to kill himself since his early twenties. This moment had been inevitable.

"Darrick...it's Mya," she said softly, hoping to reach Darrick's buried consciousness. "You're not alone. Don't be afraid." She slipped her hand into his still one and gave it a gentle squeeze. "Angelo is here. You need to get better so you can see him. He's come a long way to talk to you." It was a small lie but honesty was overrated when standing next to a dying man.

There was no response, no change, not that she expected one, but if she were going to hope for a miracle, she figured she ought to dream big.

"Darrick," Angelo said. "I'm going to catch who did this to you. I promise. But I need your help. Only you can help us find who killed Waylon. I know you know. Help us find that person and bring them to justice."

Darrick's eyelids twitched and Mya held her breath. She looked to Angelo, and shook her head, not wanting him to get his hopes up. "It's probably just a reflex," she said. "This happens when—"

"A-ang-elo," Darrick wheezed, his eyelids seeming weighted in cement for the effort it took to raise them. Angelo leaned closer to catch the words barely making it past Darrick's lips.

"I'm here, Darrick," Angelo said. "Tell me who killed Waylon. I'm here to listen. I'll believe you."

"S-so sorry...m-my fault," Darrick gasped, a lone tear tracking down his yellowed skin. "M-my f-fault."

"It's not your fault. You were a kid, too. Tell me who did it so I can bring them in. Someone is killing people to keep something secret. What is it?" He couldn't soften the urgency in his tone and Mya found herself hanging on every word, hoping against hope that Darrick could tell them something of importance.

"W-water...it's the w-water... F-father know—" A death rattle choked off whatever else he'd been trying to say and within a heartbeat, Darrick Willets had lost his grip on life.

Alarms and monitors went off and a team rushed in. As Mya and Angelo moved to make room for the medical personnel it was hard not to feel the acute loss coupled with confusion from Darrick's last words.

"The water?" Angelo repeated, mostly to himself. "What does that mean?"

Mya wiped at the tears tracking down her cheeks, grieving for the loss of a tribal member whose spirit had walked with his best friend so many years ago, and shook her head. "I don't know," she answered. "I need to call Randy—"

"Wait," Angelo said, halting her in midstep. "He said something about his father knowing…what if he meant that whatever is happening, Randy knows why?"

Mya sniffed back tears, trying to focus. "Maybe, but someone needs to tell him that his son is dead and I'm not going to let a stranger do it."

Angelo nodded, relenting. "Of course. I'll meet you outside in the lobby."

Mya jerked a short nod and went to find a private place to call Randy Willets. In her career as an emergency-room doctor and clinic physician there were times she'd had to deliver bad news, but it never got any easier. Particularly when she was faced with the prospect of telling a parent that their child was dead, no matter their age.

She knew Randy lived with regret. This news wasn't going to lighten that burden.

Angelo had told Mya he'd wait for her in the lobby but as soon as he'd reached the empty room, he'd kept walking, right out the front doors. The bracing cold air hit his face like a damp, frigid fist and he welcomed the blow. The sensation felt real, solid, tangible and he knew how to deal with it. His face to the wind, he closed his eyes and breathed deeply the air of his homeland.

His ancestors had traveled these woods, floated down the waterways, and traded with the neighboring tribes on this soil. He hoped what peace had eluded Darrick in life had found him in death. And another part of him—a quiet and almost imperceptible part of him—hoped Waylon was there to greet his long-lost buddy, to take him where their ancestors dwelled in happiness. A song—if you could call it that—welled in his chest and fought to be free. Tears sprang to his eyes and he didn't know where they came from. He felt he needed to sing the song for Darrick, for Waylon, for Papa…even for Bunny. Their ancestors used to put their dead in a cedar canoe and set them on their return journey to Creator, the canoe ablaze until it sank in the water. They'd mourned in song, their voices rising to the heavens as one. He choked up. Where was this coming from? Was he losing his mind?

White Arrow, fly straight, fly true…

He whirled, grinding the moisture from his eyes, half-terrified that he'd see Waylon or Papa standing there, but when he turned he saw Grace and Mya exiting the hospital together. *Pull it together,* he told himself sharply. Perhaps he was losing his mind.

Mya must've sensed something was off. She came to him with worried eyes. "You okay?" she asked and he shrugged off her concern.

"Fine," he said, immediately regretting his clipped tone, but he had too much going on in his head at the moment to explain. "Did you talk to Randy?" he asked.

"Yes," she answered. "He's understandably upset."

"I'm sorry for his loss but I've got questions that he's going to answer whether he likes it or not. I'm done with chasing ghosts. I want to know what's going on and I aim to find out."

"The man just lost his son," Mya reminded him quietly. "Let's give him some time to grieve."

"I'm sorry. I can't do that. Grace and I will talk with Randy. I need you to go back to Hettie and see if she's ready to talk. I think she knows something, too. There are too many damn secrets in this tribe. It's time to flush them out."

Chapter 22

Mya found Hettie holed up at her niece's place, which wasn't far from her own little house near the river.

Hettie didn't look pleased to see her, either.

Mya exchanged looks with Hettie's niece, Faith, who simply shook her head. "She doesn't want to talk to no one," Faith said. "But I think she needs to get to the clinic. She's got a sore like Uncle Bunny had, except hers is on her leg. I'm worried."

Mya rested a hand on Faith's shoulder to reassure her, said, "I'll do what I can," then followed in the direction Hettie had disappeared. She found the older woman standing by the window, staring out at the bend in the river, a thick blanket tucked around her.

"I knew you'd come sniffing around again," she said. "Why can't you just leave things alone?"

"Because people are being killed. *Our* people, Hettie. Whatever you know you need to tell me."

"It's not going to do no good, except get me put in the ground just like my Bunny," she said with a sniff. "I'm an old woman and I shouldn't have to worry about these kinds of things. We were doing just fine until people started asking questions about things that ought to be left alone. Maybe Bunny would still be here if that agent hadn't started asking about that boy."

"Hettie, let me see the sore on your leg."

Hettie looked sharply at her, surprise in her expression until Faith came around the corner and she surmised how Mya had known. "Girl, I told you it was nothing," she growled at her niece, plainly incensed that Faith had shared her business. "It's just a sore from a scratch I got. It festered, is all."

"Same as Bunny's?" Mya asked. "That was no ordinary wound, so if yours is the same, I need to get you to the hospital. You could get blood poisoning and die."

"At least I'd be with my Bunny," Hettie said with a watery sniff. "I can't believe he's gone, the grouchy old badger."

"Auntie, please," Faith implored Hettie, true concern in her eyes. "Just let Dr. Jonson take a look real quick."

Hettie's mouth pinched, but when she saw the worry etched on her niece's face, she relented with typical ill humor. Mya didn't care as long as she got to take a look. Hettie shucked her blanket and hitched her pant leg to show Mya the seeping wound on her ankle. It looked painful and raw. Mya held back her gasp when she saw it. "When did you get this?" she asked, trying to remain cool and calm. "Around the same time as Bunny?"

Hettie shrugged. "I guess. We were down at the river. He was fishing, trying out some new lure and I was collecting river stones for my new garden. I slipped and cut myself on one of the rocks. It just never healed right.

Hurts real bad," she finally admitted, risking a glance at Mya to see what she thought.

Mya's first concern was getting Hettie to a lab to take samples. She had a terrible feeling about that wound, the same feeling she'd had when she'd seen Bunny's. As far as she knew neither Hettie nor Bunny were diabetic, which would preclude ulcerous sores due to insulin imbalances. So, why did both Hettie and Bunny have matching sores?

Darrick's last words floated into her mind.

"The water…" she murmured.

Faith stepped forward. "What about the water?"

"Don't go there," Hettie warned, fear flashing in her eyes. "They'll find out somehow and that's how Waylon died."

"They who?"

Hettie compressed her lips but clutched at Mya's hand. "Just leave it be. You're a good girl, don't let this ruin everything that you've built."

"Hettie, what's wrong with the water?" Mya asked, not allowing the unsettled lump of fear forming in her gut to show itself in her voice. "What did Waylon find out?"

Hettie squeezed her eyes shut and a tear escaped. "We just wanted to be left alone. But they started coming around, dumping stuff in the water during the high-water season… Take a sample of the water…it's in there now. It's what's killing the fish and killing the spirit of the Hoh. And it's been going on for a long time. Waylon was going to do something about it."

A sixteen-year-old boy? Mya thought incredulously, but she couldn't ignore the facts as they were appearing. Waylon had been silenced, as were Agent Hicks and Bunny, and God knows who else. That brought them back to Randy Willets and what he knew.

Mya looked to Faith. "Do you have a zippered plastic bag I could use?" Faith nodded and went to get one. Mya returned to Hettie. "I'm going to take a sample of the water. Where is the water most contaminated?" she asked.

Hettie seemed reluctant to answer but did anyway. "There's a spot over where Darrick put his tent. Where the water pools you can find a ring of brown and yellow muck. That seems to be a spot where the stuff collects that doesn't get washed out to the sea. But be careful, they've got eyes everywhere."

They? Who are they? She kept her questions to herself, but she had a feeling Hettie didn't know who was behind all this anyway. She'd save those questions for Randy. She tried to reassure Hettie with a smile. "We're going to get this figured out and no one else is going to get hurt. In the meantime, I want you to let Faith take you into the clinic. We need a sample and you need some antibiotics at the very least. That sore could turn gangrenous and then you could lose your leg."

Hettie blanched. "Lose my leg?" At Mya's nod, she gestured to Faith, saying, "I ain't losing my leg after everything I've been through. I figure I've already lost enough. Get your keys, Faith."

Faith sent a silent expression of gratitude Mya's way for convincing her aunt to get help.

But as Hettie disappeared to get properly dressed to go out, Mya said to Faith in a low voice, "Is there some place you can stay for a few days? I'm not comfortable with you two here on the river given the circumstances."

"We could stay with my mom—she moved to Port

Angeles—but Auntie and my mom don't really get along."

"Try to find a way. It's not safe right now."

"Okay," Faith agreed. "I'll find a way. My auntie… she's not as hard as she seems. Deep down, she's a very kind lady."

"I know." Mya smiled. "And you're a good niece for protecting her."

Mya took the plastic bag and headed for the river.

Angelo knocked on Randy Willet's front door while Grace did a quick perimeter check. He had time to knock twice more and for Grace to return with an all-clear before Randy opened the door, looking like hell raked over.

"I'm not up to visitors right now," he said dully, his normally neatly groomed hair completely unkempt, as if he'd just been roused from bed, and his eyes swollen as if he'd been crying. Angelo felt a momentary twinge for Randy's loss, but his son had died bearing a burden that wasn't his to bear. Angelo suspected Randy knew this, too. "Go away."

Randy tried to close the door, but Grace stopped him with the flat of her palm against the door and Angelo pushed forward, compelling the older man backward. "No, I'm sorry, I can't do that. I have questions and you, I suspect, have the answers."

Randy sent Angelo a sour glare. "You're a heartless thug with a badge," he said, but Angelo was way past taking offense. He was too focused on finding answers. He was like a hound on a scent and he smelled his quarry. "My only son died today."

At that Angelo acknowledged his loss. "I know. I'm sorry. I remember him being a good kid."

Randy's lip quivered. "He was."

"So what happened?"

The bald question was probably in bad taste but Angelo was being ruthless. Randy was vulnerable in his grief, and his guard was down. There would be no better time to squeeze him for answers.

"Get out."

"Say it like you mean it or don't waste my time. What happened to your son? And what does it have to do with my brother?"

"Waylon," Randy gasped, as if the name alone had the power to cause him pain. "Waylon..."

"What about Waylon?" Angelo demanded, sweat popping along his hairline. "What do you know?"

Randy's legs seemed to go out from under him and Grace was there to catch him and deposit him on the couch. "Maybe we ought to call for an ambulance," she said, but Angelo wasn't ready to relent.

"What is it? Darrick said you knew what was going on. Something about the water? What water? The drinking water? The river? What?" Randy paled and his skin became clammy, but Angelo was ready to scream, knowing the answers were so frustratingly close. He grabbed Randy by his collar and shook him, causing Grace to jump after him. "What killed my brother?" he yelled.

Grace yanked on his arm, but he shrugged her off with a growl. "Back off, Grace," he warned, ready to return to Randy, who was visibly shaking in his grip, but Grace wasn't one to push around and he should've remembered that.

"Stand down," Grace demanded, the steel in her voice jerking him around. "Stop and think about what you're doing."

He glared, his adrenaline pumping. "This man knows who killed my brother and why."

"This man is about to die of a heart attack," she said, not backing down. "Last time I checked, dead men don't answer questions."

Angelo returned to Randy and saw what Grace said was true. He swore under his breath before saying, "Call a damn ambulance. He's not going to die without coughing up what he knows."

Grace flipped her cell phone to her ear and made the call and Angelo, sparing one last look of disgust for Randy, stalked from the house to simmer down.

He'd lost his cool, his objectivity. Frustration unlike anything he'd ever known ate at him, biting into his calm and his professional ability until he was consumed by a roiling mass of choking rage and desperation, acting like a rookie on his first case. That wasn't him. Not by a long shot. And yet, here he was, blowing hard from the adrenaline and behaving like a wild man out for revenge, not an agent seeking justice.

Angelo nudged a rock with the toe of his shoe, trying to come back to the case with a fresh perspective. He pulled out his cell phone and dialed Mya.

She picked up and just the sound of her voice calmed him—until he heard the subtle tremor.

"Angelo, I think I may have found the source of Bunny's and Hettie's sores. There's something in the water, something that's not supposed to be there. I think it's contaminated. I've taken a sample and I'm on my way to the hospital now. But there's something else I found when I was collecting the sample and you're going to want to see it."

"What is it?"

"Well, Darrick's camp was near the sample spot and

I found some of his things. I started gathering some of his personal effects in case Randy wanted to keep them and I found some pictures hidden under his pillow."

"Pictures? What kind?"

"Really old ones. A few are of Darrick and Waylon when they were kids, but others are of people dumping something in ten-gallon drums into the water. I think Waylon and Darrick stumbled onto— Wait, what the—" Mya's voice cut off as metal crunching metal rang through the phone, causing his heart to stop.

"Mya?"

"Angelo!" Her voice sounded frantic in his ear. "Someone is trying to run me off the road!"

"Where are you?" he asked, sprinting for the car.

"Heading for the Pititchu Bridge, almost there— Oh, God, here he comes again!"

Another crunch of metal and squeal of tires and then the line went dead.

"Grace!" he shouted as he skidded around the car, jerking open the door. She appeared just as he climbed inside. "Trouble. Someone's trying to kill Mya. Keep an eye on Willets. Don't let anyone near him. This is about loose ends and he's definitely that for whoever is involved with this."

Grace acknowledged him with a firm nod before disappearing inside again, no doubt locking the door behind her.

He peeled out of the driveway and on the way dialed Sundance. "Mya's in danger. En route to the Pititchu Bridge. Situation not secure. I repeat, situation is *not* secure."

"On my way." Sundance's curt response was followed by a click. Angelo tossed his phone onto the seat and pressed the gas pedal harder.

Chapter 23

Mya slowly became aware of freezing-cold water hitting her ankles and rapidly climbing her legs. She was disoriented for a moment and took a second to realize what had happened and what kind of danger she was in.

But the shocking bite of the water filling her car snapped her into panicked action. She jerked at her seat belt—it stuck. Murky river water hit her waist and she screamed for help, still yanking on the caught belt. Whoever had run her off the road had managed to push her off right before the bridge, sending her car hurtling down the steep embankment to land nose-down in the water and she was sinking fast.

"Help!" she screamed again, the fear putting a wild shrill note to her voice. She couldn't die this way. She had too much to do still. She was too young. She wanted to be a wife, a mother, *a grandmother!*

Angelo's face flashed in her memory and she yanked

harder in desperation as tears rained down her cheeks. She took deep, gulping breaths as the water hit her chest and her purse floated by. *Nooooo!* She grabbed her purse and twisted the strap around her arm in a hopeless attempt to hold on to the important pictures inside.

She wouldn't die without having the chance to tell Angelo how much she still loved him. She couldn't let whoever was responsible for all this pain go unpunished. She thought of Iris and Sundance and how much she loved them both and how her last words to Iris had been sharp. She'd do anything to take them back. She pictured all the people in her life whom she loved and cherished and, as the water closed over her head, she took one last desperate breath and realized her time had come.

Great Spirit was calling her home.

Angelo saw the back end of Mya's car slip into the dark depths of the water and he jumped from his car and broke into a sprint. He didn't hesitate, just dove into the water.

His eyes adjusted to the water and saw Mya's limp body floating, anchored by the seat belt that had been damaged by the crash. He pulled his utility knife and activated the window breaker. The window cracked and splintered and glass shards drifted away on the current. He sliced her seatbelt and pulled her body through the open window. He dragged her from the water onto the shore, gasping for air, chilled to the bone, terrified because she was silent as the grave.

"No, Mya," he shouted, checking for a pulse. Nothing. "It's not going to end this way!"

He heard the ambulance but he started CPR on his

own. Breathing for her, he kept up resuscitation even as tears streamed down his face. It couldn't end this way, it just couldn't. Mya—his beautiful, strong, smart woman—was not meant to die choking on river water. She was meant to do amazing things in her life. To be a wife and a mother, to be the soul of their tribe.

She was meant to be *his* wife and the mother to *his* children.

Why? He wanted to scream to the heavens, to his ancestors, to Great Spirit who'd taken so much from him in his lifetime. Why would he take Mya, too?

The paramedics pushed Angelo aside and he reluctantly relinquished her body so they could work. Sundance was on their heels, his face white. "Mya?" he breathed, pain and anguish in his voice.

"Brother," Angelo stopped him, mindless of his own tears, the tribal familiarity coming to him unbidden. Sundance stared, his eyes filled with wild grief. Angelo folded him into a fierce embrace, knowing the fear Sundance felt because he was trapped in it, too. "She wasn't breathing...I'm afraid she's gone."

"We have a pulse!" the paramedic shouted and the work became a frenzy. "We have to get her to the hospital. Now!"

Sundance and Angelo broke apart and hope fluttered between them. Could it be? Another paramedic handed Angelo Mya's sodden purse, saying, "She had this wrapped around her arm," before closing Mya into the ambulance and driving away with the most precious cargo on the reservation in Angelo's opinion.

Neither Sundance nor Angelo wasted time on talk. Both bounded for their separate cars to chase the ambulance to the hospital.

* * *

A bright light blinded Mya. She shielded her eyes and turned away but warmth emanated from the light and she was so cold. She wanted to bathe herself in that warm glow, to shake off the chill seeping into her bones. She took a step toward the light but something held her back. She glanced down and saw nothing, but she felt pressure on her hand, as if an invisible presence were tethering her to this cold place. She tugged, but she remained stuck. The warmth blazed hotter, beckoning, drawing her, and tears stung her eyes. She wanted that heat, that blessed comfort. A silhouette passed through the light and she realized she wasn't quite alone, but she couldn't make out faces. People were walking into the light, so why couldn't she? She was being left behind! She pulled harder and pain erupted up her arm, causing her to yelp and stop trying to escape. Tears fell down her face. Why was she always being left behind? A familiar shape emerged from the light but stopped short of reaching Mya. The light blazed around the shape until it converged on a beloved face.

"Grandma Rachel?" she made out, the tears coming faster. She reached out to her grandmother, the woman who'd helped raise her and Sundance when their parents had died, and she was hurt when Grandma Rachel simply smiled and shook her head. "I want to be with you. I've missed you so much," she said.

Grandma Rachel radiated love from her round, soft body and Mya choked on her tears. "Please…"

Not yet.

And that tugging on her hand was strong enough this time to jerk her farther away from Grandma Rachel and that blessed heat. She cried out but the light started to dim, dwindling in on itself and taking Grandma Rachel with it, until she was alone in the cold dark of some terrible place.

But the pressure on her hand that had frightened her so much had suddenly become a comfort. She turned away from the cold and toward the presence that she couldn't see but felt acutely.

She closed her eyes and allowed the pull to draw her away. She didn't know where it was leading her, but somehow she knew it was to safety.

Angelo listened to the doctor explain what was happening to Mya, all the while keeping her hand clasped in his. He wouldn't leave her side, not to eat, not to sleep. Sheer exhaustion stole a few winks from him but even in dead slumber he kept her hand in his. He wouldn't let go. He wouldn't let anyone persuade him to leave her side.

The cold water had slowed her heart rate and, though she'd been without oxygen for approximately eight minutes, they'd been able to revive her because the cold had worked in their favor. But she'd slipped into a coma for a short time as her body had struggled to regain consciousness. That had been two days ago.

"She seems to be coming around, but I want to warn you that she might have sustained brain damage from the lack of oxygen," the doctor said, his tone grim.

Angelo wiped at the moisture on his face and returned to gaze at his beautiful woman. She looked as if she was simply sleeping, but he knew she hovered between worlds. He'd spent the last two days fervently praying to a God he'd forsaken, ancestors he'd forgotten and any other deity that might have cause to take pity on a mere, messed-up mortal with a hole in his heart at the idea of losing the only woman he'd ever loved.

And he wasn't alone. Sundance and Iris had stationed themselves at the foot of her bed as well, taking shifts by her side. He took comfort in their presence. Even Grace had poked her head in to check on him and Mya, after she'd deposited Randy Willets into a safe house for his protection for the time being. And while Angelo was sequestered with Mya, Grace ran down leads, not that there were many. The photos inside Mya's purse, although wrapped in plastic, had been partially ruined by time and then water. Grace had had them sent to the FBI labs for processing, in the hopes that the sophisticated forensic department could isolate faces for recognition. It was a long shot, but the photos were the one and only lead they'd had, and Mya had nearly died trying to get them to him. Grace had sent a biopsy of Hettie's wound to forensics as well. They were still awaiting the results, but one small stroke of good luck had found them—the results from Bunny's autopsy.

Grace had delivered the news personally.

"The man was riddled with cancer, stage four, it looks like," Grace said. "But he also had high levels of potassium chromate in his system. That's a highly toxic carcinogen, and likely what caused his cancer."

"How does a fisherman who rarely leaves the reservation come into contact with something like that? Does it occur naturally around here?"

"No," Grace said. "It's usually used in dye-manufacturing plants because of its bright red color."

"Randy Willets is part owner of a small textile plant an hour or so from here…"

Grace's mouth twitched. "That explains why he hasn't been very cooperative, but it doesn't explain who's going around popping off loose ends."

Angelo nodded and Grace gestured to Mya. "Any change?"

"None yet, but she's strong, she'll pull through," he said, forcing the confidence into his voice even though his spirit was flagging. All he had was a dogged sense that Mya wouldn't leave this world without a fight. In the meantime, he'd wait by her side and Grace would be his go-between and his muscle.

Mya's eyelids twitched and he tried not to react. The doctor had warned him that involuntary movements didn't necessarily mean anything. But each time she moved, his heart leaped just the same. This time, a soft groan escaped her lips and everyone in the room jumped.

"Do you think...?" Iris asked, the hope in her voice mirroring his own. Sundance clasped Iris's hand but leaned forward, his eyes bright.

Mya groaned again and her leg slid slowly into a different position under the blanket. "Wh-what h-happened?" she croaked, her voice hoarse and raw.

Iris hopped up to get the doctor and Sundance flanked Mya's other side while Angelo could barely speak. Tears flooded his eyes, and all he could do was smooth the hair at her crown, so delirious that she was alive and awake.

Sundance sensed he was beyond words and took the lead.

"We're so glad you're finally awake. We were afraid that you were going to leave us behind. How do you feel?"

"Groggy," she said with a faint grimace. She looked down and saw Angelo's hand tenderly holding her own. "You... I remember..." She frowned. "Um, I'm sorry.

I can't seem to think straight," she said, dropping her head against the pillow.

"Don't overdo it," Angelo said, finding his voice. "You've been through a lot."

Her breath hitched as she remembered. "Did you find who pushed me off the road?"

Angelo shook his head. "Not yet, but we will. We're getting close to finding out who's behind all this. Grace has been running down leads and we're going to find out who did this. I promise."

Iris returned with the doctor, and Angelo reluctantly moved out of the way while Mya was examined.

Angelo backed away and Sundance followed while Iris hovered close to Mya.

"When are you talking with Randy Willets?" Sundance asked in a low voice.

Angelo scrubbed his palms over his face, feeling every lost hour of sleep beneath his overwhelming relief that Mya had finally opened her eyes and seemed coherent. "He's in a safe house with Grace. I plan to go as soon as Mya seems in the clear." He looked to Sundance and noted the tensing of his jaw. "Why? You want to come with?"

"I sure as hell do," Sundance answered. "I've got a few questions of my own for the man. Seems he knows a lot more than he's saying and if he had anything to do with Mya's accident…well, let's just say he's going to get a lesson in family loyalty."

Angelo matched Sundance's grim promise with a feral smile. "You read my mind, brother."

Chapter 24

Randy Willets looked like a broken man, Angelo thought as he stared him down.

"What's in the water, Randy?" Angelo asked, deceptively calm. No response, but Randy shifted his gaze away. Angelo rapped the table with his knuckles, demanding Randy's full attention. "No, you don't have the option of checking out of this conversation. I want answers and I'm going to get them."

Grace came forward. "You own a textile company, right?" When Randy remained silent she continued, "I did a little research and found that your textile company uses potassium chromate in the dying process of certain fabrics. Funny thing about that stuff, it's highly toxic. A known carcinogen."

Angelo leaned forward. "And you know what's funny about that? Bunny Roberts had a bad sore on his arm, much like the sore his wife, Hettie, has on her ankle.

Turns out they're chemical burns. From potassium chromate. And that stuff doesn't just pop up naturally like mushrooms under a log. Any idea how a fisherman and his wife happened to get burned by a highly toxic chemical?"

Sweat beaded Randy's lip and he began to shake. "Y-you're supposed to be keeping me safe, not grilling me like a criminal," he said, but his voice had lost its bite. In fact, he seemed downright pathetic. If Angelo had had an ounce of compassion for Randy Willets, it had died the minute someone tried to kill Mya.

"We collected a sample near where your son camped on the river—it was contaminated with potassium chromate. Imagine that," Grace said.

Sundance came forward. "And guess what we found in Mya's purse? Old pictures...lots of them. Of people dumping something into the river, something that's definitely not biodegradable."

"What are you saying?" Randy said, trying to bluff.

"Your records with the EPA state your company is over its legal limit for toxic and hazardous waste, which means you've had to sell off quantities to other companies who haven't reached their limit, but you haven't had a buyer in years. So where's the waste going, Randy?" Grace asked.

"I don't have to answer—"

Angelo jumped in, his blood running hot. "You're right, don't bother, because I think I know. You've been dumping it into the Hoh River during peak flow in the spring because the Hoh flows into the ocean and who's going to know? Well, someone found out, didn't they? Someone like Waylon." He got into Randy's face. "You killed my little brother in cold blood, didn't you? Didn't you! He was just a boy! Who are you to play God? To take his life when he had so much to live for?"

Randy's eyes welled and he seemed to dissolve into a shaking, babbling mess of a man. Angelo stepped back as Randy dropped his head into his hands to sob noisily. "I never meant for that to happen. It wasn't supposed to happen. No one was supposed to get hurt. It seemed a small enough risk and we had so much to lose," Randy said, tripping over his own words. "We had to offload the chemicals or else the fine was going to cripple the business. We couldn't stop production and couldn't find a buyer for the stuff. The Hoh flows so fast during the spring, we thought no one would be the wiser."

"How'd Waylon find out?"

"I don't know, the fish, I guess. The first dump killed off some fish and crawdads. I told Darrick to stay away from the river during the peak flow, but he never listened. It was supposed to be a warning shot, meant to scare the kids, but I was nervous and my shot went wild, hitting Waylon. I never knew he'd been taking pictures. I just thought to scare him off." His eyes watered. "I never meant to kill him. I swear."

Angelo had always thought that when he stared into the eyes of his brother's killer he'd have to restrain himself to keep from strangling him with his bare hands, but he felt nothing. Not pity, not rage. Both had seeped out of him as he stared at the broken man before him. Guilt and regret had done the work for him and there was no glory in beating a man when he couldn't fight back.

"Is that why you've been knocking off the others? Tying up loose ends?" Grace asked.

Randy shook his head vehemently, his lips white.

"I'm not killing anyone. Waylon's death was my fault, but I didn't touch the rest."

"If not you, then who?" Sundance asked.

"Joseph Reynolds," Angelo answered for Randy, seeing the man's cold, calculating eyes in his memory. "Your cousin and business partner, right?"

Defeated, Randy could only nod. "He's been holding Waylon's death over my head for years. I told him no more, that we couldn't keep dumping the stuff in the Hoh, but he said it was the perfect solution to our problem and told me if I didn't go along with it, he'd make sure someone found out about Waylon. I couldn't take the risk...and I was afraid. Joseph is ruthless. I didn't put it past him to do whatever it took to get his way. Then, when that agent started poking around...I don't know, he said he'd take care of it. I didn't know—but I should've figured—that he was going to do something drastic."

"And by then you were in so deep, you couldn't get out," Grace surmised, and Randy jerked a nod as he wiped at his nose. Grace shared a look with Angelo. "I'll get an arrest warrant for Joseph Reynolds as well as a search warrant for his property."

Angelo nodded and Grace took off, wasting little time. For all they knew, Joseph was hightailing it to Mexico by this point.

"I never meant to hurt anyone," Randy whispered. "I just wanted to survive."

"Yeah, well, so did the people you killed with your greed," Angelo said, pushing away. "Cuff him, Sundance. I've heard enough from this scum."

Sundance jerked Randy's arms around the back and cuffed him tightly, causing Randy to grunt in pain. Then, as Sundance was leading him out to his vehicle,

Randy stopped to stare at Angelo, resentment in his eyes. "You think I haven't been punished all these years? You're wrong. I've lived with guilt every day, and now my only son is dead."

"You'll get no sympathy from me," Angelo stated flatly. "If it weren't for you, my brother would still be alive. I don't really care if you suffer regret. But I do hope you rot in prison."

Sundance jerked Randy around and stuffed him into his SUV. Justice—for Waylon, at least—had been served. Now, they had to lock down Randy's squirrelly accomplice.

But first, Angelo needed to see Mya again. He needed to reassure himself that she was alive and well. She was his True North and he couldn't believe it had taken him this long to figure that out.

Angelo, Grace and Sundance entered the swanky office building in Seattle that Joseph Reynolds used to handle business operations for his and Randy Willet's textile business and startled Joseph as he appeared to be packing.

"Going somewhere?" Angelo asked with perfect calm. Joseph stilled then straightened and met Angelo's stare without flinching.

"What's this about?" Joseph had the balls to ask as if affronted by their busting into his business and bypassing appropriate channels.

"Oh, I think you know," Angelo said. "You're under arrest for murder."

The man chuckled but the sound was forced. "I don't appreciate your humor."

Angelo widened his stance. "I'm not laughing."

Grace tossed a warrant to the desk. "This gives us

permission to search the premises as well as take you into custody for the murder of Darrick Willets."

Joseph paled and actually stumbled a little as his butt found his chair. Angelo came forward. "You left your DNA all over that disguise you wore to sneak into Darrick's room to deliver the fatal overdose, and as soon as we search your financials I'm sure we'll find the money you paid the sharpshooter to kill Bunny Roberts and special agent Hicks, because you sure as hell don't look as if you have that kind of skill. I'm curious, though, why'd you dirty your hands to kill your own family member? I'd have thought you'd have handed off that job."

Caught, Joseph remained silent while Grace jerked him out of the chair and cuffed him.

"Cat got your tongue or are you shy all of sudden?" Angelo asked, his tone hard.

"I want a lawyer," Joseph said stonily, refusing to meet Angelo's stare.

"All right. Keep your secrets. I've uncovered the ones that matter. You're going to prison. Enjoy your very long incarceration. I know I'll sleep better knowing you're behind bars."

"You don't know a thing about what it takes to run a business in this economy. We scrabble for every dime. We employ hundreds of people, some of whom are your tribe members who've had to leave the reservation because there's no money to feed their families, and here you judge me because I did what I had to do to survive and protect not only my livelihood but that of hundreds of employees? How nice a luxury," Joseph ended on a sneer that made Angelo want to put his fist through the man's mouth.

Angelo stepped forward, his fists clenched, but he

kept himself from punching Reynolds. Still, he said, "You can shove that sanctimonious crap. You poisoned the very water that gave your tribe life. You killed the fish, sickened Hettie and Bunny, and God knows who else. You're a parasite, willing to suck the blood of others, so don't try and paint yourself into anything other than what you are. Get him out of my sight," he growled.

"On your feet," Grace said, jerking Reynolds up and propelling him forward. "You're going for a ride, courtesy of the government."

Sundance came to Angelo and clasped his shoulder. "You did it," he said, approval deep in his tone. "You found justice for Waylon and the others. He can rest now, and so can you."

Angelo looked to Sundance and knew he was staring at a man who was integrity personified, someone he'd be blessed to call his brother. But would Sundance welcome him in the same way?

"I'm going to marry her," he said simply.

Sundance nodded gravely, then broke into a grin. "It's about time. She's been waiting long enough for you to come home. Her heart has always belonged to you, even if I didn't want that for her at the time. But you've changed. You're the man your grandfather had hoped you'd be. I'd be honored to call you my brother."

Angelo's breath caught in his throat.

"And I, you."

Sundance smiled. "Then it's agreed. Now you just have to convince Mya."

"I think I may have an idea on how to do that."

Sundance clapped Angelo on the shoulder and they left together while Grace transported the prisoner.

Each step felt lighter as Angelo realized he'd finally

achieved closure and he was ready to move on—only this time it was in the right direction.

Mya grew stronger every day and Angelo had been a constant source of encouragement, whether it was coaxing her to eat her pudding or sternly seeing to it that she got her nap. She loved the attention, but she had to get out of this place, and pronto.

Which is exactly what she had in mind when Angelo walked in and found her dressed and waiting.

"What are you doing?" he exclaimed, not the least bit happy to see her up and about on her own.

"I'm perfectly fine. I feel like a prisoner. I need real food," she said without apology. "Besides, I can rest better in my own bed rather than this creaky hospital bed."

"I could arrange a different bed," he offered helpfully, a suggestion she waved away with distaste. He frowned. "The doctor said—"

"I'm a doctor and I say I'm fine. I didn't break any bones or suffer a concussion. I'm fine."

"You were legally dead for eight minutes," Angelo said.

"And now I'm completely alive and bored out of my brain. Now, either take me home or I will find someone who will." She wasn't taking no for an answer. If she stayed one more minute in this hospital bed she was going to become one with the mattress. "What's it going to be?"

"You're a terrible patient," he grumbled and she grinned.

"I know. And I'm starved for something juicy and artery-clogging, like a fat steak or a ridiculously big hamburger with French fries smothered in ketchup."

"Got your appetite back, I see," he said.

"Yes, I did, and I'm not eating another tray of hospital food. I just won't. So will you take me somewhere with good food?"

"Of course," he said, smiling, but she could tell fear for her health held him back. She took a bold step toward him and wrapped him in a tight embrace before lifting on her toes to press a kiss to his lips, startling him, but she was pleased when his arms automatically folded around her. "You don't fight fair," he murmured against her mouth.

"I never said I did."

"Okay, but we're not staying out late. You're back in bed right after dinner. The doctor said you need to take it easy."

She figured she wasn't going to win that argument so she agreed for the sake of keeping the peace, but inside she was restless. Being dead for eight minutes had given her a new perspective and a thirst for taking what she needed from life. And she needed Angelo. She wouldn't live without him. Not that she couldn't, just that she refused to. They'd already lost out on fifteen years together, she wasn't about to lose out on another moment.

"I want a baby," she said, nearly causing him to trip on his own feet. "I want *your* baby. Will you give me a baby, Angelo?"

Angelo's mouth dropped open and something that looked a lot like joy and fear all wrapped in one expression filled his face. She smiled, knowing how he felt. "You don't have to answer right this second—"

He startled her when he crushed her to him, claiming her mouth with an intensity reserved for souls lost and suddenly found, kissing her to within an inch of her life, until she was drowning in happiness.

He broke the kiss, reluctantly it seemed, but he murmured with heart-breaking honesty, "The answer is *yes.* Yes, Mya. God, *yes.* I want you to be the mother of my children. And to be my wife."

Tears broke loose as the well she'd been stuffing all her hopes and dreams into burst and flowed over her.

She jerked a happy nod, admitting with a laugh, "Good. Because I wasn't going to take no for an answer and it would've been pretty awkward when I tied you to my bed to get what I want."

Angelo's mouth tipped in a sensual grin that made her want to eat him up as he said, "That's my woman. Strong and willful. Just the way I like her. Now, let's make some babies." He gave her a playful push toward the door with a pinch to her rear and Mya thought she'd never heard a more endearing statement.

Well, with the exception of what he'd said to her after putting away Randy Willets and Joseph Reynolds. "I want to be the man you think I can be. It's time for me to come home."

Epilogue

One year later...

Angelo settled into his restored cedar canoe, the cold of the morning air deceiving. He knew once he started paddling and the sun hit the sky full-force, any lingering chill would be burned away. He ran his fingers through the water, feeling his brother's spirit beside him.

Porter slapped him on the shoulder good-naturedly. "You ready for this?" he asked.

Angelo laughed ruefully. "We'll see."

They had a small crew compared to some of the other participants in the Canoe Journey, but as he saw Mya on the shore, her large rounded belly protruding beautifully, he knew she was proud of him. He was making this journey in honor of his ancestors and his family. He'd lived too long shunning his heritage and all it entailed. He was ready to embrace who he was, and that included embarking on the annual Canoe Journey. Mya had wanted to go, too, but he'd persuaded her to cheer him on from the sidelines in deference to her pregnancy. His son grew in her belly and he'd take no chances with the safety of their child.

He'd taken his rightful place as Tribal Chief and although he remained an agent, he wore dual hats now. He put the needs of his tribe in the forefront of his mind, fighting for tribal land so they could grow strong again. He wanted to teach his son to cherish his Native heritage and to have pride in his ancestry.

He would do all the things he'd been meant to do and he'd do them with honor and with Mya by his side.

His eyes misted as he stared out across the shimmering water of his homeland.

White Arrow had finally flown straight and true, returning to where he belonged—his native country.

* * * * *

Harlequin®

ROMANTIC
SUSPENSE

COMING NEXT MONTH

Available August 30, 2011

You can find more information on upcoming
Harlequin® titles, free excerpts and more at
www.HarlequinInsideRomance.com.

HRSCNM0811

REQUEST YOUR FREE BOOKS!
2 FREE NOVELS PLUS 2 FREE GIFTS!

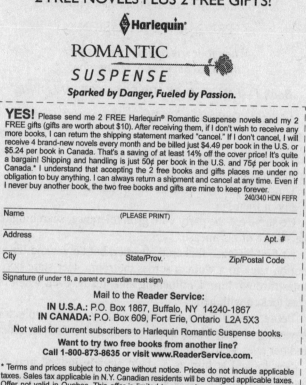

❧ Harlequin®

ROMANTIC
SUSPENSE

Sparked by Danger, Fueled by Passion.

YES! Please send me 2 FREE Harlequin® Romantic Suspense novels and my 2 FREE gifts (gifts are worth about $10). After receiving them, if I don't wish to receive any more books, I can return the shipping statement marked "cancel." If I don't cancel, I will receive 4 brand-new novels every month and be billed just $4.49 per book in the U.S. or $5.24 per book in Canada. That's a saving of at least 14% off the cover price! It's quite a bargain! Shipping and handling is just 50¢ per book in the U.S. and 75¢ per book in Canada.* I understand that accepting the 2 free books and gifts places me under no obligation to buy anything. I can always return a shipment and cancel at any time. Even if I never buy another book, the two free books and gifts are mine to keep forever.

240/340 HDN FEFR

Name	(PLEASE PRINT)	
Address		Apt. #
City	State/Prov.	Zip/Postal Code

Signature (if under 18, a parent or guardian must sign)

Mail to the **Reader Service:**
IN U.S.A.: P.O. Box 1867, Buffalo, NY 14240-1867
IN CANADA: P.O. Box 609, Fort Erie, Ontario L2A 5X3

Not valid for current subscribers to Harlequin Romantic Suspense books.

Want to try two free books from another line?
Call 1-800-873-8635 or visit www.ReaderService.com.

* Terms and prices subject to change without notice. Prices do not include applicable taxes. Sales tax applicable in N.Y. Canadian residents will be charged applicable taxes. Offer not valid in Quebec. This offer is limited to one order per household. All orders subject to credit approval. Credit or debit balances in a customer's account(s) may be offset by any other outstanding balance owed by or to the customer. Please allow 4 to 6 weeks for delivery. Offer available while quantities last.

Your Privacy—The Reader Service is committed to protecting your privacy. Our Privacy Policy is available online at www.ReaderService.com or upon request from the Reader Service.

We make a portion of our mailing list available to reputable third parties that offer products we believe may interest you. If you prefer that we not exchange your name with third parties, or if you wish to clarify or modify your communication preferences, please visit us at www.ReaderService.com/consumerschoice or write to us at Reader Service Preference Service, P.O. Box 9062, Buffalo, NY 14269. Include your complete name and address.

HRS11B

New York Times *and* USA TODAY *bestselling author*
Maya Banks presents a brand-new miniseries

PREGNANCY & PASSION

When four irresistible tycoons face
the consequences of temptation.

Book 1—ENTICED BY HIS FORGOTTEN LOVER

Available September 2011 from Harlequin® Desire®!

Rafael de Luca had been in bad situations before. A crowded ballroom could never make him sweat.

These people would never know that he had no memory of any of them.

He surveyed the party with grim tolerance, searching for the source of his unease.

At first his gaze flickered past her, but he yanked his attention back to a woman across the room. Her stare bored holes through him. Unflinching and steady, even when his eyes locked with hers.

Petite, even in heels, she had a creamy olive complexion. A wealth of inky-black curls cascaded over her shoulders and her eyes were equally dark.

She looked at him as if she'd already judged him and found him lacking. He'd never seen her before in his life. Or had he?

He cursed the gaping hole in his memory. He'd been diagnosed with selective amnesia after his accident four months ago. Which seemed like complete and utter bull. No one got amnesia except hysterical women in bad soap operas.

With a smile, he disengaged himself from the group

around him and made his way to the mystery woman.

She wasn't coy. She stared straight at him as he approached, her chin thrust upward in defiance.

"Excuse me, but have we met?" he asked in his smoothest voice.

His gaze moved over the generous swell of her breasts pushed up by the empire waist of her black cocktail dress.

When he glanced back up at her face, he saw fury in her eyes.

"Have we *met?*" Her voice was barely a whisper, but he felt each word like the crack of a whip.

Before he could process her response, she nailed him with a right hook. He stumbled back, holding his nose.

One of his guards stepped between Rafe and the woman, accidentally sending her to one knee. Her hand flew to the folds of her dress.

It was then, as she cupped her belly, that the realization hit him. She was pregnant.

Her eyes flashing, she turned and ran down the marble hallway.

Rafael ran after her. He burst from the hotel lobby, and saw two shoes sparkling in the moonlight, twinkling at him.

He blew out his breath in frustration and then shoved the pair of sparkly, ultrafeminine heels at his head of security.

"Find the woman who wore these shoes."

Will Rafael find his mystery woman?
Find out in Maya Banks's passionate new novel
ENTICED BY HIS FORGOTTEN LOVER
Available September 2011 from Harlequin® Desire®!

Harlequin®

ROMANTIC
SUSPENSE

NEW YORK TIMES BESTSELLING AUTHOR

RACHEL LEE

The Rescue Pilot

Time is running out…

Desperate to help her ailing sister, Rory is determined
to get Cait the necessary treatment to help her fight
a devastating disease. A cross-country trip turns into
a fight for survival in more ways than one when their plane
encounters trouble. Can Rory trust pilot Chase Dakota
with their lives, and possibly her heart?

**Look for this heart-stopping romance in September
from *New York Times* bestselling author Rachel Lee
and Harlequin Romantic Suspense!**

Available in September wherever books are sold!

Dear Reader,

One of my favorite themes is that of redemption. I find the more a character has screwed up, the more opportunity there is for emotional growth. I think Angelo Tucker is one of those characters who will always have a fond place in my heart because he was forced to shoulder a mountain of guilt based on a decision made in his youth that had far-reaching consequences. Angelo's redemption is both sweet and fierce, which is perfect because that sums up his character at his core.

I did a lot of research for this series as the Hoh tribe is an actual tribe in Washington State; however, I did take some poetic license with setting and certain aspects of the reservation as this is a fictitious story and not grounded in reality. I hope you enjoy the ride!

Hearing from readers is a special joy. Please feel free to drop me a line via email through my website at www.kimberlyvanmeter.com or through snail mail at Kimberly Van Meter, P.O. Box 2210, Oakdale, CA 95361.

Kimberly

"It doesn't have to be this way," Angelo said, spreading his hands in a gesture of peace.

Mya paused, her silhouette outlined against the milky light of the parking lot lamp. She cut a striking figure in the brisk spring night, her breath curling before her. "It is what it is and we should leave it that way," she replied and then climbed into her car before he could offer a rebuttal.

He watched as she drove away, wishing for a glimpse into her private thoughts. He wondered what he'd see.

His instincts told him he wouldn't like it.

Mya had always been a terrible liar. Her feelings reflected quite clearly in her strong gaze and, assuming that aspect of her hadn't changed, there was no mistaking how she felt about him.

And it wasn't nice.

* * *